AF596521

The Bloodstone Alpha

The Blood Moonstone, Volume 2

D. Kepko

Published by D. Kepko, 2024.

This is a work of fiction. Similarities to real people, places, or events are entirely coincidental.

THE BLOODSTONE ALPHA

First edition. December 17, 2024.

Copyright © 2024 D. Kepko.

ISBN: 979-8230314431

Written by D. Kepko.

Table of Contents

Chapter 1

The village of Grey Hollow slept under the eerie glow of a blood-red moon. Its cobblestone streets were silent, save for the occasional rustle of leaves or the distant hoot of an owl. Deep in the heart of the village, Gizmo sat on the edge of a crumbling stone fountain, rubbing his temples as Boston and Julz argued nearby.

"I'm just saying," Julz hissed, pacing back and forth, "if you hadn't ignored the warning signs, we wouldn't be in this mess!"

"And I'm saying," Boston growled, his broad shoulders tense, "that maybe if someone hadn't been obsessed with collecting those stupid herbs, we wouldn't have been out there at all!"

"Enough," Gizmo muttered, his voice barely audible. But when neither of them stopped, he slammed his fist against the fountain's edge. "I said enough!"

Julz and Boston fell silent, turning to look at him. Even in the dim light, Gizmo's pale complexion was hard to miss. Sweat beaded on his forehead, and his hand clutched his forearm, where crimson streaks spidered out from beneath a hastily wrapped bandage.

"You're not looking too good, Giz," Boston said, his tone softening.

"No kidding," Gizmo replied, his usual sarcasm dulled by pain. "It is a werewolf bite, Boston. You do not exactly walk it off."

Julz knelt in front of him, her sharp eyes scanning the wound. "We need to act fast. The venom's spreading quicker than I thought."

"Tell me something I don't know," Gizmo groaned.

Julz ignored him, pulling a worn leather book from her satchel. She flipped through its yellowed pages, her fingers trembling slightly. "The only way to stop the transformation is with the Lunar Petal. It is a rare flower that grows deep in the Wraithewood Forest."

Boston snorted. "The Wraithewood? That place is crawling with every nightmare imaginable. We would barely last an hour in there."

Julz shot him a withering glare. "Do you have a better idea? Because unless you have got a magical cure in your back pocket, the forest is our only option."

Boston opened his mouth to argue but stopped when Gizmo let out a low growl of pain.

"Fine," Boston said, running a hand through his dark hair. "We will go. But if this goes sideways, I am blaming you."

The trio set out within the hour, the oppressive stillness of the Wraithewood looming before them like a wall. The forest was alive with an unnatural energy, its gnarled trees twisting into grotesque shapes under the moonlight.

"Stay close," Boston murmured, his crossbow at the ready.

Julz walked beside Gizmo, keeping a close eye on him. Every so often, he would stumble, and she would catch him before he fell. "How are you holding up?" she asked.

"Fantastic," Gizmo replied with a weak smile. "I give it five stars. Would recommend to a friend."

Julz rolled her eyes but could not hide the flicker of worry in her expression.

As they ventured deeper, the air grew colder, and an unnatural fog crept along the ground. Boston stopped suddenly, raising a hand to signal silence.

"What is it?" Julz whispered.

Boston did not answer. His sharp eyes scanned the shadows, and his grip tightened on his crossbow.

Then they heard it—a low, guttural growl that sent shivers down their spines.

"We're not alone," Boston muttered.

The growl grew louder, and from the darkness emerged a pair of glowing red eyes. A massive werewolf stepped into the moonlight, its fur matted with blood, its claws gleaming like knives.

"Run," Boston commanded, his voice low and urgent.

But the werewolf moved faster. It lunged at them, claws outstretched. Boston fired his crossbow, the bolt striking the creature's shoulder. It let out a deafening roar but did not stop.

Julz grabbed Gizmo's arm and pulled him back. "Come on!"

The trio sprinted through the forest; the werewolf hot on their heels. Branches clawed at their faces, and the ground seemed to shift beneath their feet.

"This way!" Boston shouted, leading them toward a narrow path.

But as they ran, Gizmo's strength gave out. He tripped, crashing to the ground. The werewolf was on him in an instant, its jaws snapping inches from his face.

"Gizmo!" Julz screamed, throwing a vial of glowing liquid at the creature. The vial shattered, and the liquid hissed as it hit the werewolf's fur, making it recoil.

Boston grabbed Gizmo and hauled him to his feet. "Move!"

They did not stop running until the growls faded into the distance. When they finally stopped to catch their breath, Gizmo collapsed against a tree, his chest heaving.

"That... was too close," he panted.

Julz knelt beside him, her face pale. "We cannot keep this up. We need to find the Lunar Petal—and fast."

Boston nodded grimly. "Then let us move. The clock's ticking."

As the blood moon hung high above them, the trio pressed on, unaware of the even greater dangers that lay ahead. The fog thickened as they ventured deeper into the Wraithewood Forest, cloaking their surroundings in an oppressive gloom. Every sound—a snapping twig, a distant rustle—felt amplified, making their nerves hum with tension.

Gizmo leaned heavily on Julz, his strength waning with every step. The crimson streaks from the bite mark on his arm had spread farther, winding like sinister vines toward his shoulder. His breaths came shallow and ragged.

"Talk to me, Gizmo," Julz urged, her tone brisk but laced with worry. "How is your arm? Any feeling?"

"It's... tingly," he replied, his voice faint. "Like pins and needles, but on fire. You know, the fun kind of pain."

Julz frowned and shot Boston a look. "We don't have long."

Boston glanced over his shoulder, scanning the path behind them. "I know," he said grimly. "Let's pick up the pace."

The Whispering Path

As they pressed on, the forest seemed to shift around them. The trees grew taller and closer together, their twisted branches forming archways that led them deeper into shadow. Strange whispers echoed through the air, faint and unintelligible, like voices carried on the wind.

"Okay, that's new," Boston muttered, gripping his crossbow tighter.

Julz froze mid-step, her eyes narrowing. "Those are not just whispers. They are spells. The forest is trying to confuse us."

Gizmo let out a weak laugh. "Great. As if the werewolf was not enough, now the trees are against us."

Boston ignored the quip, pointing to the faint glow of moonlight ahead. "We stick to the light. If we lose sight of it, we are done for."

The whispers grew louder as they moved forward, taking on an almost taunting quality. Gizmo's legs wobbled, and Julz struggled to keep him upright.

"I can't..." Gizmo began, his voice barely audible. "I can't keep going."

"Yes, you can," Julz snapped, shaking him lightly. "The Lunar Petal is close. Just hold on a little longer."

But even as she spoke, Gizmo's knees buckled. He collapsed to the ground, clutching his chest. His eyes were wide, golden flecks beginning to shimmer in their depths.

Boston dropped to his side, panic flashing across his usually stoic face. "What's happening?"

"The venom's accelerating," Julz said, her voice tight. "We're out of time."

A GLIMMER OF HOPE

Before they could react, a soft, silvery light broke through the fog ahead. The whispers faltered, fading into the background. Julz's heart leapt.

"That has to be it," she said, pointing toward the light.

Boston hesitated. "And what if it's a trap?"

"It doesn't matter!" Julz snapped. "It's our only chance!"

Without waiting for a response, she hauled Gizmo to his feet and half-dragged him toward the light. Boston cursed under his breath but followed, his crossbow at the ready.

As they approached, the light grew brighter, revealing a small clearing in the forest. At its center stood a single flower, its petals glowing softly like moonlight captured in bloom. Surrounding it were jagged rocks and the charred remains of what looked like fallen adventurers.

"That's it," Julz whispered. "The Lunar Petal."

Gizmo stirred, his voice barely above a whisper. "It's... beautiful."

But before they could step into the clearing, a low, guttural growl rumbled from the shadows. Boston turned sharply, raising his crossbow.

"We've got company," he said.

Emerging from the darkness was another werewolf, this one even larger than the first. Its fur shimmered with a strange, ethereal glow, and its eyes burned with a fierce intelligence.

"Fantastic," Boston muttered. "The guardian."

A Desperate Gamble

The werewolf prowled forward, its lips curling back to reveal razor-sharp teeth. It did not charge immediately, instead circling them as though sizing up its prey.

"We can't fight that thing," Julz whispered, clutching a small vial of shimmering liquid from her satchel.

"Then what do you suggest?" Boston asked, not taking his eyes off the creature.

Julz glanced at Gizmo, then at the flower. An idea began to form, reckless but their only option.

"I'll distract it," she said, handing the vial to Boston. "You get the flower and give him this."

Boston stared at her like she had lost her mind. "That's suicide."

"I know," Julz said, her expression grim. "But if we don't do something, Gizmo's as good as gone."

Before Boston could argue, Julz stepped into the clearing, her heart pounding. She uncorked another vial from her satchel and hurled it at the werewolf. The glass shattered on impact, releasing a burst of blinding light.

The werewolf howled in fury; its glowing eyes fixed on Julz.

"Come on, you overgrown mutt!" she shouted, backing toward the trees. "Let's dance!"

As the werewolf charged after her, Boston did not hesitate. He sprinted into the clearing, grabbed the Lunar Petal, and crushed it into the vial Julz had given him.

"Gizmo, drink this!" Boston ordered, forcing the mixture to Gizmo's lips.

Gizmo coughed and sputtered, but he swallowed the potion. Almost immediately, the crimson streaks on his arm began to recede, and his breathing steadied.

Boston turned back to the clearing just in time to see Julz narrowly dodge the werewolf's claws.

"Boston!" she yelled. "A little help here?"

With Gizmo on the mend, Boston raised his crossbow, aimed carefully, and fired.

The silver bolt struck true, piercing the werewolf's heart. It let out a final, bone-chilling howl before collapsing in a heap.

Julz stumbled back, her face pale but triumphant. "Told you I had it under control," she said, brushing dirt off her jacket.

Boston rolled his eyes. "You're insane, you know that?"

"Maybe," Julz replied with a smirk. "But it worked."

As dawn began to break, the trio stood in the clearing, battered but alive. The Lunar Petal had saved Gizmo—for now. But as they looked back at the twisted forest, they knew their journey was far from over.

This was just the beginning.

Chapter 2

The trio emerged from the Wraithewood Forest just as the first light of dawn streaked across the horizon. The golden rays cast a warm glow over the landscape, but none of them felt the relief they had expected. The fight in the forest had left them battered, bruised, and uneasy.

Gizmo leaned against a tree, catching his breath. Though the venom had been neutralized, he still looked pale and drawn. His usual snark was muted, his golden-flecked eyes darting nervously toward the forest behind them.

"Is it... gone?" he asked, his voice unsteady.

Boston, still clutching his crossbow, glanced back into the trees. The Wraithewood loomed dark and silent, but something about its stillness was unsettling. He nodded slowly. "For now."

Julz dropped her satchel on the ground and sank down beside it, wiping the dirt and blood from her hands. "Let us not test our luck by sticking around to find out. We need to get back to Grey Hollow."

"Back to Grey Hollow?" Gizmo said with a weak laugh. "The place where a werewolf nearly ate me alive in the first place? Sounds cozy."

Julz shot him a glare. "We need to regroup, Gizmo. Restock supplies. Figure out what is really going on with that bite."

Gizmo's grin faltered. "What do you mean? You gave me the cure. I am fine now... right?"

Julz hesitated, exchanging a glance with Boston.

"Right?" Gizmo pressed, his voice rising slightly.

"We stopped the venom from turning you into a full werewolf," Julz said carefully. "But the Lunar Petal does not undo everything. There could be... side effects."

"Side effects?" Gizmo repeated, his eyes narrowing. "Like what? Claws? Fangs? Random urges to howl at the moon?"

"We don't know," Boston said bluntly. "That's why we need to go back and figure it out."

Gizmo groaned, rubbing his temples. "Great. So, I might still be a ticking time bomb."

Julz stood and crossed her arms. "You are alive, Gizmo. Let us start with that and take it one step at a time."

THE ROAD BACK

The path to Grey Hollow was eerily quiet, the usual chirping of birds and rustling of leaves absent. Even the wind seemed reluctant to stir.

Gizmo trudged along in silence, his steps heavier than usual. Boston took the lead, his crossbow slung across his back but his hand never far from it. Julz walked between them, her sharp eyes scanning their surroundings.

"You're unusually quiet," Julz said to Gizmo after a while.

He shrugged. "Just... thinking."

"About?"

"About how a normal night at the tavern turned into *this,*" he said, gesturing at the forest behind them. "About how I got bitten, almost turned into a monster, and now have 'side effects' to look forward to. You know, the usual."

Julz softened, her voice losing its usual sharpness. "You did not ask for this, Gizmo. But we will figure it out. We always do."

Boston glanced back over his shoulder. "As touching as this is, keep your guard up. Something is off."

Julz frowned. "You're just paranoid."

"Maybe," Boston said, his tone grim. "But I'd rather be paranoid than dead."

A Sudden Ambush

They were nearing the outskirts of Grey Hollow when the attack came. Without warning, the ground beneath them exploded in a cloud of dirt and debris. Gizmo was thrown backward, landing hard against a tree.

"Gizmo!" Julz shouted, but she barely had time to react before a shadowy figure emerged from the dust.

It was humanoid, but its features were distorted, like a nightmare given form. Its skin was dark and cracked, its eyes glowing faintly red. long claws extended from its hands, and its movements were unnervingly quick.

"What the hell is that?" Boston growled, raising his crossbow.

"A shadow wraith," Julz said, pulling a dagger from her belt. "I thought they didn't leave the forest!"

"Apparently, it didn't get the memo," Boston said, firing a bolt. The projectile struck the creature in the chest, but it barely flinched.

The wraith lunged at Julz, its claws slashing through the air. She dodged to the side and retaliated with a quick slash of her dagger, the blade glowing faintly as it connected with the creature's arm. The wraith screeched, its form flickering like smoke.

"Magical weapons work!" Julz shouted.

"Great!" Boston yelled. "Too bad I don't have one!"

The wraith turned its attention to Gizmo, who was struggling to stand. It moved with unnatural speed, closing the distance in a heartbeat.

"Gizmo, move!" Julz screamed.

But Gizmo did not need her warning. His body moved on instinct, faster than he thought possible. He ducked under the wraith's attack and lashed out with his fist. To his shock, his hand crackled with a faint golden energy as it connected with the wraith's chest. The creature let out a high-pitched scream and dissolved into black mist.

Silence fell over the group.

"What... just happened?" Gizmo asked, staring at his hand.

"That's a good question," Julz said, her eyes wide.

A NEW MYSTERY

They reached Grey Hollow just as the sun fully rose, painting the village in warm, golden light. But the warmth did little to ease the tension among the trio.

Julz led them to a small, hidden workshop tucked behind the main square. The space was cluttered with shelves of ancient books, jars of strange ingredients, and various tools for potion-making and spell craft.

"Sit," Julz ordered, pointing to a stool as she began rifling through her supplies.

Gizmo sat obediently, his mind still reeling from what had happened. "So... about the glowing hand thing?"

"I'm working on it," Julz muttered, pulling out a thick tome and flipping through its pages.

Boston leaned against the wall; arms crossed. "We need answers, Julz. Fast. That thing out there was not random."

Julz did not look up. "I know. Shadow wraiths are drawn to dark magic—or powerful transformations. Which means..."

"Which means they're drawn to *me,*" Gizmo finished, his voice hollow.

Julz stopped flipping through the book and met his gaze. "We don't know that for sure."

"Don't we?" Gizmo said bitterly. "First, I get bitten by a werewolf, then I develop some weird golden energy powers, and now shadow wraiths are popping out of the ground. Connect the dots, Julz."

Boston stepped forward. "If they are after Gizmo, we need to find out why—and fast. Whatever is happening to him, it is bigger than just a werewolf bite."

Julz nodded slowly, her expression serious. "Then we need help. There is someone who might know more."

"Who?" Gizmo asked.

Julz hesitated. "The Oracle of Emberveil."

Boston groaned. "Of course. Because why wouldn't this already insane journey take us to the most dangerous place imaginable?"

Gizmo sighed, rubbing his temples. "Guess we're not getting that rest after all."

And so, their journey took another dark turn. The Oracle of Emberveil was a figure of legend and fear, said to dwell in a cursed ruin far from Grey Hollow. If anyone could unravel the mystery of Gizmo's transformation, it would be her. But the path ahead was fraught with peril—and their time was running out.

Chapter 3

The sun had barely climbed above the rooftops of Grey Hollow when the trio prepared to leave. Julz moved with sharp efficiency, packing vials, herbs, and her leather-bound journal into her satchel. Boston checked his crossbow, ensuring it was loaded and ready for whatever horrors awaited them on the road to Emberveil.

Gizmo, however, sat slumped on a crate, staring at his hands. Every so often, he flexed his fingers, as if expecting the golden energy to flare to life again.

"Stop overthinking it," Julz said without looking up.

"Easy for you to say," Gizmo replied. "You're not the one glowing and attracting shadow monsters."

Julz tightened the straps on her bag and glanced at him. "No, I am the one keeping you alive, so maybe cut the self-pity. We do not have time for it."

Boston smirked. "She has got a point. Brooding is not going to help us get to the Oracle."

Gizmo scowled but said nothing.

THE FIRST SIGNS

The road to Emberveil was long and winding, cutting through dense forests and rocky terrain. The closer they got, the more the landscape changed. The trees grew twisted and gnarled, their branches resembling claws reaching for the sky. The air grew colder, and a strange mist clung to the ground, swirling around their feet as they walked.

"This place is worse than the Wraithewood," Boston muttered, his eyes scanning the shadows.

"It's the curse," Julz explained, her voice hushed. "The ruins of Emberveil have been steeped in dark magic for centuries. The closer we get, the more we will feel it."

"Fantastic," Gizmo said, shivering as a chill ran down his spine. "I always wanted to visit a cursed ruin."

"Keep your sarcasm in check," Boston growled. "We need to stay focused."

Julz suddenly stopped, holding up a hand. "Wait."

The group froze. The forest was unnaturally silent, the kind of silence that made your skin crawl.

"What is it?" Boston asked, his voice low.

Julz did not answer immediately. She knelt, examining the ground. The dirt was disturbed, as though something heavy had passed through recently.

"Tracks," she whispered. "Big ones. Too big to be human."

Boston tightened his grip on his crossbow. "How fresh?"

Julz glanced around, her sharp eyes scanning the surroundings. "Fresh enough to worry about."

As if on cue, a low growl echoed through the trees.

"Here we go again," Gizmo muttered, his pulse quickening.

The Stalker in the Mist

The growl grew louder, reverberating through the forest. A figure emerged from the shadows; its hulking form barely visible through the mist. It was a creature unlike any they had encountered before—part wolf, part shadow, its body shifting and flickering as though it was not entirely solid.

"Another werewolf?" Gizmo asked, backing up instinctively.

"Not exactly," Julz said, her voice tight. "That is a Shadebeast. They are drawn to powerful magic—and they are relentless."

The Shadebeast let out a bone-chilling howl and charged.

Boston fired his crossbow, the bolt striking the creature in the shoulder. It staggered but did not stop, its glowing eyes locked on Gizmo.

"Why is it always me?" Gizmo shouted, diving out of the way as the creature swiped at him with its massive claws.

"Because you're glowing like a damn beacon!" Julz yelled, throwing a vial at the Shadebeast. The glass shattered on impact, releasing a burst of light that made the creature recoil with a furious snarl.

Boston loaded another bolt, aiming for the beast's head. "Keep it busy!"

Julz dodged another swipe and slashed at the creature with her dagger, the blade glowing faintly as it connected. The Shadebeast howled in pain, its form flickering more violently.

"Now, Boston!" Julz shouted.

Boston fired, the bolt piercing the creature's skull. The Shadebeast let out one final, earsplitting screech before dissolving into a swirl of shadow and mist.

The forest fell silent once more.

A Growing Threat

Julz wiped her blade on her sleeve, her breathing heavy. "That shouldn't have happened."

"What do you mean?" Gizmo asked, still catching his breath.

"Shadebeasts don't roam this far from cursed areas," Julz said, frowning. "Something is wrong. They are being drawn to us—or to you."

Boston turned to Gizmo; his expression grim. "She is right. Whatever is happening to you, it is getting worse."

"Great," Gizmo said, throwing his hands in the air. "First werewolves, now shadow creatures. What is next? A dragon?"

Julz ignored his outburst, already digging through her satchel for a map. "We need to move faster. The closer we get to the Oracle, the more dangerous this is going to become."

Boston nodded. "Agreed. Let us pick up the pace."

THE RUINS OF EMBERVEIL

Hours later, the trio finally reached the outskirts of Emberveil. The cursed ruins loomed before them, an imposing collection of crumbling towers and jagged spires wrapped in thick, swirling mist. The air was heavy with the stench of decay and the crackling energy of old magic.

"This place gives me the creeps," Gizmo said, shivering.

"Stay close," Julz said, her voice steady but tense. "The Oracle doesn't take kindly to visitors, and the ruins are full of traps and worse."

Boston raised his crossbow, his eyes scanning the shadows. "Let's get this over with."

As they stepped into the ruins, the ground beneath them seemed to shift, and the air grew colder. Strange whispers echoed around them, faint and unintelligible, just like in the Wraithewood.

"Julz," Gizmo said nervously, "are those more spells?"

Julz nodded. "Defensive wards. The Oracle does not like uninvited guests."

"Wonderful," Gizmo muttered.

They moved cautiously through the ruins, avoiding the glowing runes etched into the stone and the occasional shifting shadow that seemed to follow them.

Finally, they reached the center of the ruins—a massive, circular chamber with a glowing pool of water at its center. A figure stood at the edge of the pool, shrouded in a tattered black cloak.

The Oracle.

"You seek answers," the figure said, its voice echoing unnaturally. "But beware—knowledge comes with a price."

Julz stepped forward, her voice steady. "We are willing to pay it. Our friend has been cursed, and we need to know how to stop it."

The Oracle turned, revealing a face that seemed both ancient and ageless, its eyes glowing faintly. "Very well. Step forward, cursed one, and let me see the truth of your fate."

Gizmo hesitated, his stomach twisting with dread.

"Go," Julz urged gently. "We're here with you."

Taking a deep breath, Gizmo stepped toward the Oracle, his heart pounding. Whatever truth awaited him, he knew there was no turning back.

Chapter 4

Gizmo's feet felt heavier with each step, as though the air around him grew thicker the closer he got to the Oracle. The glowing pool beside the figure pulsed softly, casting eerie reflections on the crumbling walls of the chamber. Julz and Boston watched from a safe distance, weapons at the ready, their expressions a mix of concern and determination.

The Oracle extended a pale, withered hand. "Give me your hand, cursed one, and let me peer into the essence of your affliction."

Gizmo hesitated, glancing back at his friends. Julz gave him a sharp nod, her confidence unshaken.

"Right," he muttered under his breath, stepping forward and placing his trembling hand in the Oracle's. The touch was icy, sending a jolt through his arm as the Oracle's glowing eyes flared brighter.

The chamber darkened, the light from the glowing pool intensifying as shadows stretched and writhed around them. A faint hum filled the air, growing louder until it was almost deafening. Gizmo felt a strange pull in his chest, as if something deep within him was being unraveled.

"You have been marked," the Oracle intoned, its voice reverberating like an echo in a vast canyon. "The bite is not merely a curse but a tether—a fragment of ancient power seeking to awaken."

"Awaken?" Gizmo croaked; his voice barely audibles over the hum.

"The werewolf's venom carries with it more than transformation," the Oracle continued. "It carries a piece of the First Wolf—a primal being of unimaginable strength and fury. This essence is now bound to you."

Gizmo's knees buckled, but the Oracle's grip held him upright. "Bound to me? What does that mean?"

"It means," the Oracle said, its glowing eyes locking onto his, "that you are no longer entirely mortal. The wolf within you is not just a beast—it is a fragment of divinity. And it will not rest until it is whole."

The Prophecy

The Oracle released Gizmo's hand, and he staggered back, catching himself against the edge of the glowing pool. His heart pounded in his chest as he tried to process the words.

"So... what? I am some kind of vessel for this First Wolf?" he asked, his voice trembling.

The Oracle tilted its head. "Not a vessel. A spark. The wolf's essence within you can grow, ignite, and consume—or it can be extinguished. But beware: others will seek you. Some to protect, others to exploit, and many to destroy."

Julz stepped forward, her dagger still in hand. "Is there a way to stop this? To sever the bond?"

The Oracle's gaze shifted to her, its eyes narrowing. "The bond cannot be severed without great cost. To remove the wolf's essence is to risk unraveling the mortal life it clings to. But there is another path—one that requires strength, cunning, and sacrifice."

Boston stepped closer; his tone sharp. "What's the other path?"

"The fragment within you can be controlled, harnessed," the Oracle said, turning back to Gizmo. "You must seek the Lupine Codex, an ancient text containing the rites and rituals of the First Wolf's lineage. Only through these rites can you master the beast within."

Gizmo rubbed his temples. "Master it? You mean... live with it?"

"Yes," the Oracle replied. "But be warned: the path to mastery is treacherous. The Codex is hidden in the Ashen Vault, a place where the First Wolf's power lingers. Many have sought it, but none have returned."

"Of course they haven't," Gizmo muttered. "Why would anything be easy?"

The Rising Threat

As the Oracle's words settled over the group, the chamber began to tremble. The glowing pool darkened, its light dimming as cracks appeared in the floor.

"The bond stirs," the Oracle said, its voice growing urgent. "The First Wolf's essence senses its exposure and calls forth its servants. You must leave this place—now."

The ground beneath them shook violently, and a deafening roar echoed through the ruins. Shadowy figures began to materialize at the edges of the chamber, their forms flickering like smoke.

"Not again," Boston growled, raising his crossbow.

"Run!" Julz shouted, grabbing Gizmo's arm, and pulling him toward the exit.

The trio sprinted through the ruins, dodging falling debris and the claws of the shadow creatures that pursued them. The air was thick with the stench of sulfur, and the whispers that had once been faint now roared like a cacophony in their ears.

"This way!" Julz shouted, leading them down a narrow corridor that opened into a crumbling staircase.

Boston fired his crossbow over his shoulder, striking one of the shadow creatures and causing it to dissolve into mist. "They're not letting up!"

Gizmo stumbled but caught himself, his legs burning as he pushed forward. His hands crackled faintly with golden energy, the power within him responding to the danger.

"Whatever you're doing, Gizmo, figure it out fast!" Boston yelled.

"I'm trying!" Gizmo shouted back; his voice tinged with panic.

A Narrow Escape

They burst out of the ruins just as a massive explosion rocked the structure behind them. The shadow creatures stopped at the threshold, unable to cross the ancient wards that protected the perimeter.

Gasping for breath, the trio collapsed onto the grass outside.

"Well," Gizmo panted, staring up at the darkening sky. "That was... awful."

Julz sat up, her face pale but determined. "We have our answers now. The Codex is our only chance."

Boston groaned, pushing himself to his feet. "Let me guess—it's in another cursed deathtrap, right?"

"Pretty much," Julz said with a grim smile.

Gizmo let out a humorless laugh, wiping sweat from his brow. "Perfect. Just perfect."

As the trio regained their composure, the Oracle's words echoed in Gizmo's mind: *The path to mastery is treacherous. The First Wolf's essence will not rest until it is whole.*

He clenched his fists, the faint golden energy flickering to life once more. The road ahead was uncertain and dangerous, but one thing was clear: if they were going to survive, he would need to embrace the power within him—and learn to control it.

The journey to the Ashen Vault had begun.

Chapter 5

The road to the Ashen Vault was one rarely traveled; its dangers so notorious that even the most desperate wanderers avoided it. Stretching deep into the Wildlands—a vast, untamed expanse of jagged cliffs, dense forests, and ancient ruins—the journey promised peril at every turn. Yet, the trio pressed on, the Oracle's warning ringing in their ears.

Gizmo walked at the rear, his eyes darting nervously to the shadows around them. He could still feel the faint hum of power coursing through his veins, an unsettling reminder of the wolf's essence that now lived within him.

Boston led the group, his crossbow always at the ready. "I will feel better once we are out of these woods. It is too quiet."

"Too quiet?" Gizmo asked, glancing around. "I thought quiet was a *good* thing."

"Not here," Julz said, adjusting the straps of her satchel. "The Wildlands are not empty. If you cannot hear anything, it means the predators are near."

"Great," Gizmo muttered. "Nothing like impending doom to keep the blood pumping."

The First Challenge

By mid-afternoon, the forest began to change. The trees grew taller and more twisted, their gnarled branches reaching across the narrow path like skeletal fingers. Strange, glowing fungi clung to the trunks, casting an eerie blue light over the underbrush.

"Stay sharp," Julz said, her voice low.

As they continued, a faint rustling noise echoed from somewhere ahead. Boston held up a hand, signaling the group to stop.

"What is it?" Gizmo whispered.

"Something's moving up there," Boston replied, squinting into the gloom.

Julz pulled out a small vial from her satchel, shaking it until it began to glow faintly. "Light will give us the advantage. If it is what I think it is, they do not like bright things."

A low growl echoed through the forest, followed by the sound of twigs snapping. From the shadows emerged a pack of creatures, their sleek, black bodies blending almost seamlessly with the darkness. Their eyes glowed red, and their mouths were filled with sharp, jagged teeth.

"Voidstalkers," Julz hissed.

Boston readied his crossbow. "What do we do?"

Julz handed the glowing vial to Gizmo. "Keep them at bay with this. They hate light."

"What about you two?" Gizmo asked, his voice trembling.

"We fight," Julz said, drawing her dagger, its edge glowing faintly with enchanted runes.

Boston fired the first shot, his bolt striking one of the Voidstalkers square in the chest. It yelped and dissolved into a plume of black smoke, but the rest of the pack surged forward.

"Here we go!" Julz shouted, leaping into the fray.

Gizmo stood frozen for a moment, the vial glowing brightly in his hand. One of the creatures turned its attention to him, snarling as it lunged. On instinct, he threw the vial, which shattered at the Voidstalker's feet. The burst of light sent the creature skittering back, growling in frustration.

"Nice throw!" Julz called out, slashing at another Voidstalker.

Gizmo barely had time to feel proud before another creature pounced at him. His hands crackled with golden energy, and without thinking, he thrust his palm forward. A burst of light erupted from his hand, sending the Voidstalker flying into a tree.

"Did you see that?" Gizmo shouted, his adrenaline surging.

"Focus, Gizmo!" Boston barked, reloading his crossbow.

Aftermath

The battle was over within minutes, but it felt like hours. The Voidstalkers dissolved into smoke one by one until the forest was silent again.

"Everyone okay?" Julz asked, panting as she wiped blood from her blade.

"Still breathing," Boston said, slinging his crossbow over his shoulder.

Gizmo leaned against a tree, his hands still tingling from the energy he had unleashed. "I guess I am a weapon now. Great."

Julz approached him, her expression serious. "You are getting stronger. Whatever is inside you, it is adapting to the threats we are facing."

"Yeah, but is that a *good* thing?" Gizmo asked, his voice uncertain.

Julz did not answer, and the silence spoke volumes.

A Dangerous Bargain

As night fell, the trio set up camp in a small clearing, their fire casting flickering shadows on the surrounding trees.

Julz sat with her journal, sketching runes, and jotting down notes. Boston kept watch, his sharp eyes scanning the darkness. Gizmo sat by the fire, staring into the flames.

"I keep thinking about what the Oracle said," Gizmo said, breaking the silence.

"About the Codex?" Julz asked, not looking up from her notes.

"About the cost," Gizmo replied. "What happens if we do not find it? What happens if we do?"

Julz set down her pen and looked at him. "If we do not find it, the wolf's essence will consume you. You will lose control, and..."

"And I'll become a monster," Gizmo finished, his voice flat.

Julz nodded. "But if we find it, you might have a chance to control it. To use it instead of letting it use you."

"Might?" Gizmo repeated. "Not exactly reassuring."

Boston turned from his watch post. "It is the best shot you have got, Giz. You want to give up now, fine, but do not expect us to stick around when the wolf takes over."

"Boston," Julz warned, but Gizmo held up a hand.

"He's not wrong," Gizmo said quietly. "If I cannot stop this, I am a danger to everyone. Including you two."

Julz placed a hand on his shoulder. "We are not letting that happen. We are in this together, Gizmo. All the way."

The fire crackled between them; the silence heavy with unspoken fears.

Somewhere in the distance, a wolf howled, its mournful cry sending chills down their spines.

The Ashen Vault awaited, and with it, the answers they desperately needed—and the dangers they feared most.

Chapter 6

The wind carried the scent of rain and earth, a sharp contrast to the heaviness that lingered in the safehouse. Amara sat by the fire, her fingers absentmindedly tracing the patterns on her blade. The revelations about the Bloodstone weighed on her mind, intertwining with a gnawing sense of urgency.

Kael leaned against the cabin wall; his crimson gaze distant. For all his cocky confidence, she could see the tension in his jaw, the way his hands flexed as if preparing for a fight. The room was quieter now, Elias having retreated into a back chamber, leaving them with the two wolves by the hearth, who remained unnervingly silent.

Finally, Amara broke the silence. "So, what's our next move?"

Kael's gaze snapped to hers, his expression unreadable. "We head north. The seals Elias mentioned are scattered, and the closest is near the Frostshade Cliffs."

She raised an eyebrow. "Frostshade? Sounds inviting."

"It's not," Kael said dryly. "The cliffs are treacherous, and the path is often guarded by rival packs and worse. But it is where we will find the first anchor point for the seal."

Amara frowned. "You make it sound like we're walking into certain death."

"Not certain," he replied, a faint smirk tugging at his lips. "Just probable."

She rolled her eyes but could not suppress a small smile. "Great. So, when do we leave?"

Kael straightened; his tone serious. "At first light. For now, you need to rest."

Amara opened her mouth to argue but closed it when she caught the look in his eyes—protective yet firm. She was not sure whether to feel comforted or irritated by his concern.

"Fine," she said, rising from her spot. "But don't think for a second I'm letting you handle all of this on your own."

"I wouldn't dream of it," Kael said, his voice carrying a note of genuine admiration.

She retreated to a corner of the cabin where a small cot had been set up, the Bloodstone's warmth still a steady pulse against her side. Sleep did not come easily; her mind churned with questions, doubts, and the unshakable sense that her world was on the brink of something catastrophic. The morning came with a pale light filtering through the cracks in the cabin walls. Amara awoke to the sound of hushed voices and the distinct aroma of coffee brewing. She rubbed the sleep from her eyes and joined Kael and Elias near the fire.

"We need to move quickly," Elias said, handing Kael a rolled map. "The Frostshade Cliffs are days away, and the longer the Bloodstone remains exposed, the more it will attract."

Kael studied the map, nodding. "We will take the northern pass. It is the fastest route."

"And the most dangerous," Elias warned.

Kael shrugged. "Since when have we played it safe?"

Amara crossed her arms. "Shouldn't we be considering safer options? Or at least a plan that does not involve walking into enemy territory?"

Elias gave her a pointed look. "This is not a mission for the faint of heart, hunter. If you are looking for guarantees, you will not find them here."

Her jaw tightened. "I am not looking for guarantees. Just a little common sense."

Kael smirked. "Do not worry. I will keep you alive."

"Gee, thanks," she muttered.

Elias stepped closer; his amber eyes serious. "The Bloodstone chose you for a reason, Amara. That reason will reveal itself in time, but until then, you need to trust Kael—and yourself. The road ahead will not be easy, but it is the only one we have got."

She nodded, the weight of his words settling over her like a shroud. "I'll do what needs to be done."

Kael's expression softened, a flicker of respect in his gaze. "Then let's get moving."

The journey north began under a slate-gray sky, the forest thick with the scent of damp earth and pine. Kael led the way in wolf form, his movements fluid and unerring. Amara followed close behind, her senses sharp for any signs of danger. The Bloodstone's warmth felt more pronounced now, as if responding to the tension in the air.

Hours passed in relative silence until Kael abruptly halted, his ears twitching. Amara froze, her hand instinctively going to her blade.

"What is it?" she whispered.

Kael shifted back into human form; his expression grim. "We're being followed."

Amara's heart raced. "Rogues?"

"Worse," he said. "Hunters."

Her blood ran cold. "Hunters? Like me?"

Kael shook his head. "Not like you. These are mercenaries—wolves and humans—who hunt for power, wealth, and whatever else they can take. And they will kill anyone who stands in their way."

Amara gripped her blade tighter. "How many?"

Kael tilted his head, listening. "At least three. Maybe more."

Her stomach churned, but she forced herself to focus. "What's the plan?"

Kael's lips curled into a predatory grin. "We give them a reason to regret following us."

As he shifted back into wolf form, Amara felt a surge of determination. Whatever challenges lay ahead, she would face them head-on. Together with Kael, she would protect the Bloodstone—and whatever secrets it held—from those who sought to abuse its power.

The first clash was about to begin.

Chapter 7

The forest closed in around them, shadows dancing in the early morning light as Amara and Kael prepared for the inevitable. The faint rustle of leaves behind them was the only warning of their pursuers—mercenaries who thrived on chaos and greed. Amara's grip on her blade tightened, her senses sharpening to a razor's edge.

Kael's wolf form melted into the underbrush, his dark coat blending seamlessly with the surroundings. He moved with a predator's grace, circling around their stalkers. Amara felt the Bloodstone's warmth against her side, a steady pulse that seemed to synchronize with her heartbeat. It was not fear she felt but an intense clarity—a readiness for what was coming.

The first mercenary stepped into the clearing. He was a towering figure, his armor a patchwork of leather and metal, a longsword resting casually on his shoulder. His eyes gleamed with cruel amusement as he surveyed the area.

"You can come out now," he called, his voice a low growl. "We know you're here."

Amara stepped forward, her blade glinting in the light that filtered through the trees. "Didn't anyone ever teach you to knock?" she said, her tone edged with defiance.

The mercenary's lips curled into a sneer. "Bold for someone who's outnumbered."

Amara smirked. "I've handled worse."

Before the mercenary could respond, a shadow exploded from the underbrush. Kael struck with feral precision, his wolf form barreling into a second mercenary who had been creeping toward Amara's flank. The man cried out as Kael's teeth sank into his shoulder, the sound cut short as they both disappeared into the thicket.

The clearing erupted into chaos. Two more mercenaries emerged, one wielding a crossbow, the other dual daggers. Amara pivoted, her blade clashing against the daggers in a burst of sparks. She moved instinctively, her training taking over as she parried and struck, forcing her opponent back.

The crossbowman took aim, but before he could fire, Kael reappeared, shifting mid-leap. He landed in human form, slamming the mercenary to the ground with a brutal efficiency. Blood spattered the forest floor as Kael's claws raked across the man's chest.

Amara's opponent lunged, his daggers flashing in the light. She sidestepped, her blade slicing through his defenses and cutting a deep gash along his arm. He hissed in pain, retreating with a snarl. Amara did not give him the chance to recover. With a swift, decisive strike, she disarmed him, sending his daggers clattering to the ground.

"Yield," she demanded, her blade at his throat.

The man glared at her but nodded, his hands raised in surrender. Amara glanced toward Kael, who had subdued the crossbowman. The first mercenary—the leader—still stood, his longsword raised and eyes calculating as he surveyed the battlefield.

"Impressive," he said, his tone grudgingly respectful. "But you are out of your depth. That stone you are carrying is worth more than your lives. Hand it over, and we will let you walk away."

Amara snorted. "You really think that's going to work?"

Kael stepped beside her, his crimson eyes blazing. "You made a mistake coming after us. Walk away while you still can."

The leader chuckled, a cold, humorless sound. "Suit yourselves."

He lunged, his longsword slicing through the air with deadly precision. Kael met him head-on, their blades clashing in a thunderous impact. Amara moved to flank him, her movements swift and precise, but the leader was skilled, his strikes calculated to keep them both at bay.

The fight dragged on, the forest echoing with the sounds of steel and growls. Amara's breath came in sharp bursts, her muscles burning as she pressed the attack. Finally, she saw an opening. As the leader turned to block Kael's strike, Amara lunged, her blade slicing through his guard and plunging into his side.

The leader staggered, his sword falling from his grasp. Kael delivered the final blow, his claws raking across the man's throat. The mercenary crumpled to the ground, lifeless.

Amara bent over, catching her breath as the adrenaline ebbed. Kael wiped the blood from his hands, his expression grim.

"Are you okay?" he asked, his voice softening.

She nodded, straightening. "I will live. What about you?"

He gave her a small, reassuring smile. "I've had worse."

They surveyed the scene, the forest now eerily silent. Kael searched the leader's body, pulling out a folded piece of parchment. He scanned it, his expression darkening.

"What is it?" Amara asked.

Kael handed her the parchment. "It is a bounty. For us. And the Bloodstone."

Her stomach twisted as she read the words. The reward was exorbitant, enough to attract every mercenary, rogue, and hunter in the region.

"This isn't going to stop," she said, her voice barely above a whisper.

Kael's eyes met hers, a fire burning within them. "No, it is not. But we will face it together."

Amara nodded, her resolve hardening. The Bloodstone's warmth pulsed against her side, a constant reminder of the burden she carried. The path ahead was treacherous, but she would not back down. Not now. Not ever.

Chapter 8

The forest had long since swallowed the sun's warmth, leaving a chill that seeped into Amara's bones. As she and Kael pressed forward, the silence felt heavy, as if the trees themselves were holding their breath. The map Kael had recovered from the mercenaries' leader guided them deeper into the unknown, promising answers but offering little comfort.

"We're close," Kael said, his voice low. "The markings indicate a village beyond this ridge. If the rumors are true, they have been hiding secrets about the Bloodstone for generations."

Amara's fingers brushed against the Bloodstone, the faint hum of its power resonating through her. "What kind of secrets?"

Kael hesitated. "Not the kind people share willingly. Be ready for anything."

The climb was steep, and by the time they reached the ridge, Amara's muscles burned. But the sight before them made her forget her fatigue. Nestled in a valley below was a village that looked untouched by time. Wooden huts with thatched roofs clustered together, smoke curling lazily from chimneys. A stone tower rose at the village's center, its weathered surface etched with symbols that seemed to shimmer faintly in the moonlight.

Kael tensed beside her, his crimson eyes scanning the scene. "Stay close," he said, his tone brooking no argument.

As they descended, the village's peaceful facade began to fray. Shadows moved where none should have been, and the air grew thick with a tension that set Amara's nerves on edge. When they entered the village, the streets were eerily empty, save for a lone figure waiting near the tower.

The man was tall and wiry, his gray hair pulled back into a loose braid. He wore a simple robe, but the staff in his hand radiated an unmistakable power. His piercing blue eyes locked onto Amara as they approached.

"You carry the Bloodstone," he said, his voice a blend of awe and wariness. "Why have you come here?"

Amara exchanged a glance with Kael before stepping forward. "We need answers. The Bloodstone—what is it? Why does everyone want it?"

The man's gaze softened, but his grip on the staff tightened. "You seek knowledge, but knowledge comes at a price. The Bloodstone is more than you realize. It is both a gift and a curse, a beacon, and a weapon."

Kael growled low in his throat. "We do not have time for riddles. If you know something, tell us."

The man sighed, gesturing for them to follow him into the tower. Inside, the air was thick with the scent of aged parchment and herbs. Shelves lined the walls, crammed with books and artifacts that seemed to hum with dormant power. At the center of the room was a circular table carved with the same shimmering symbols that adorned the tower.

"The Bloodstone was created long ago, during a war between the Elemental Clans," the man began. "It holds the essence of their combined power—fire, water, earth, and air. Together, these elements could shape the world or destroy it."

Amara's breath caught. "Why would anyone create something so dangerous?"

"Desperation," he said simply. "The Clans were on the brink of annihilation. The Bloodstone was meant to unite them, to bring balance. But instead, it became a source of conflict, its power too great for any one clan to wield. They hid it away, hoping its legacy would fade."

Kael's expression darkened. "But it did not. And now it is drawn hunters, mercenaries, and gods know what else."

The man nodded. "The Bloodstone chooses its bearer. It has chosen you," he said, looking at Amara. "But its choice will not go unchallenged. There are those who believe its power should be theirs alone."

"Who?" Amara demanded.

"A shadowed force known only as the Crimson Order," the man said, his voice dropping to a whisper. "They believe the Bloodstone's power is their birthright. They will stop at nothing to claim it."

Amara's heart sank. The bounty, the mercenaries, the danger that seemed to follow her every step—it all made sense now.

"How do we stop them?" she asked.

The man's expression turned grim. "To stop them, you must first understand the Bloodstone's true nature. It will test you, push you to your limits. If you fail, it will consume you. But if you succeed, its power will be yours to command."

Kael stepped closer to Amara, his presence steadying her. "We will face it. Together."

The man's gaze lingered on Kael, as if measuring his resolve. Finally, he nodded. "Then you must prepare. The Crimson Order will come for you, and when they do, they will bring their full strength. But you are not without allies. This village owes its survival to the Bloodstone. Its people will fight for you, if you give them reason to believe."

Amara squared her shoulders, the weight of the Bloodstone suddenly feeling lighter. "We'll give them a reason," she said, determination hardening her voice.

The man smiled faintly. "Then may the elements guide you."

As they left the tower, Amara felt the Bloodstone's warmth flare against her side, stronger than ever. The fight ahead would be brutal, but for the first time, she felt the stirrings of hope. Together, they would face whatever shadows came their way.

Chapter 9

The village stirred with quiet unease as the sun crept over the horizon, bathing the valley in a soft golden glow. Amara and Kael stood in the heart of the square, surrounded by wary villagers whose eyes spoke of both fear and hope. The air was charged with unspoken questions as the elder from the tower, introduced as Oran, prepared to address them.

Oran raised his staff, and the murmurs fell silent. "People of Althea," he began, his voice resonating through the square, "the time has come to fulfill our ancient vow. The Bloodstone has returned to its chosen bearer, and with it, the chance to protect our world from the darkness that seeks to consume it."

The crowd's reaction was mixed—some faces lit with determination, while others showed only fear. A stout man near the front, with a face lined by years of hardship, stepped forward.

"You speak of ancient vows, Oran," he said gruffly, "but what of the risks? The Crimson Order is no myth. They have destroyed entire villages for less. Are we to bring their wrath upon ourselves?"

Oran's gaze was steady. "The wrath of the Crimson Order will come regardless. They will not stop until the Bloodstone is theirs. But if we stand together, we can protect not just our village, but the balance of the elements themselves."

Kael stepped forward, his presence commanding immediate attention. "He's right," he said, his voice a low growl. "The Order will not give up. But I have fought them, and I have survived. If we work together, we can do more than survive. We can win."

The stout man's gaze shifted to Amara. "And what of you, girl? You are the one they are after. What makes you worthy of our trust?"

Amara swallowed hard, feeling the weight of every eye on her. She stepped forward, forcing herself to meet his gaze. "I didn't ask for this," she said, her voice firm despite the nerves twisting in her gut. "But the Bloodstone chose me, and I will not run from that. I have seen what the Crimson Order can do, and I will fight them with everything I have. But I cannot do it alone. I need your help."

A murmur rippled through the crowd, but before anyone could speak, a young woman pushed her way forward. Her auburn hair was tied back, and a bow was slung across her back. "I'll fight," she said. "If the Bloodstone chose her, then it is our duty to protect her. To protect all of us."

Her declaration seemed to ignite something in the villagers. One by one, others stepped forward, voicing their support. The stout man hesitated, then nodded gruffly. "Fine. If we are doing this, we had better be ready."

Oran's eyes gleamed with pride. "Then we will prepare. Gather your weapons and supplies. Tonight, we meet in the hall to plan our defenses."

As the villagers dispersed, Amara felt a hand on her shoulder. She turned to see Kael, his expression unreadable.

"You handled that well," he said.

She smiled faintly. "I'm not sure they're convinced."

"They'll fight," he said. "And that's what matters."

The hall was packed by nightfall, the villagers' faces lit by the flickering glow of lanterns. Oran stood at the head of the room; a map of the valley spread out before him. Amara and Kael flanked him, their presence lending weight to his words.

"The Crimson Order will come swiftly once they learn the Bloodstone is here," Oran said. "We must use the terrain to our advantage. The forest provides natural cover, and the tower offers a vantage point for archers."

The auburn-haired archer, who had introduced herself as Lyra, nodded. "We can set traps along the main path. Slow them down and pick them off before they reach the village."

Kael leaned over the map, his clawed finger tracing a line through the forest. "They will likely send scouts ahead. We need patrols to intercept them."

"And what of the Bloodstone?" the stout man asked. "If they get their hands on it, all of this will be for nothing."

Amara placed a hand over the stone, feeling its pulse beneath her fingertips. "I'll keep it safe," she said. "But if it comes to it, I will fight. This is my responsibility."

The room fell silent, the weight of her words sinking in. Finally, Oran spoke. "Then it is decided. We prepare for battle. May the elements guide us all."

As the villagers began their preparations, Amara stepped outside, needing a moment to clear her mind. The night was crisp, the stars bright against the inky sky. She leaned against the tower, her thoughts swirling with doubt and determination.

Kael joined her, his presence as steadying as ever. "You're doing fine," he said.

She glanced at him, a small smile tugging at her lips. "You always say that."

"Because it's true," he replied. "You've got more fight in you than anyone I've met."

Before she could respond, a faint rustle in the forest caught their attention. Kael's hand went to his sword, and Amara felt the Bloodstone pulse in warning.

"We're not alone," he said, his voice a low growl.

Amara's heart pounded as they scanned the tree line. The shadows seemed to shift and swirl, and for a moment, she thought she saw glowing red eyes staring back at her.

The Crimson Order had arrived.

Chapter 10

The Crimson Order wasted no time. As dawn's light barely began to touch the valley, their attack came swift and brutal. A scout's horn blared from the edge of the forest, shattering the fragile calm. Amara was jolted awake by the sound, her heart racing as she grabbed the Bloodstone and rushed out of her hut.

Kael was already in the square, sword drawn, barking orders to the villagers. "Archers to the tower! Fighters to the barricades! Everyone else, take shelter!"

Amara sprinted to his side, the Bloodstone thrumming against her chest. "How many?"

Kael's crimson eyes flicked to her briefly before returning to the treeline. "Too many. But we will hold them."

Oran appeared, his staff glowing faintly with power. "The traps will slow them, but we need to hold the line long enough for the Bloodstone to attune itself. Amara, you must stay close to the tower. Its magic will amplify the stone's connection to you."

"I'm not hiding," Amara protested.

Kael's grip tightened on his sword. "You are not. You are protecting the one thing that could save us all. Trust us to fight."

She hesitated but nodded, stepping back toward the tower. Lyra, the archer with auburn hair, joined her, bow in hand. "I will cover you. Do not do anything reckless."

The first wave came swiftly. The traps Lyra had set along the forest path snapped into action, sending nets flying and explosive powders igniting. Cries of pain and anger echoed through the air as the Order's soldiers stumbled into the open. But their numbers were overwhelming, and soon they were upon the village.

Kael roared as he met the first attackers, his blade slicing through armor and flesh. The villagers, armed with spears, pitchforks, and whatever weapons they could find, fought with a ferocity born of desperation. Lyra's arrows flew true, each shot finding its mark.

Amara watched from the tower's base; her hands clenched around the Bloodstone. She felt its power growing, a steady pulse that seemed to synchronize with her own heartbeat. But it was not enough. She could see the strain on Kael's face, the desperation in the villagers' movements. They needed more.

"Focus," Oran said, his voice calm despite the chaos. He stood beside her, his staff glowing brighter now. "The Bloodstone is a conduit, but you must guide it. Close your eyes. Feel its power and direct it to those who need it most."

Amara nodded, shutting out the sounds of battle. She let her breathing steady, her thoughts reaching for the Bloodstone's energy. Slowly, she felt it respond, its warmth spreading through her chest and into her limbs. She imagined Kael, Lyra, and the villagers, their courage and determination lighting up in her mind like beacons.

A surge of power rippled outward. The villagers, locked in combat, seemed to stand taller, their strikes more precise. Lyra's arrows glowed faintly as they struck their targets with unerring accuracy. Kael, now a whirlwind of destruction, fought with renewed vigor, his blade carving a path through the enemy.

But the Crimson Order was relentless. For every soldier that fell, two more seemed to take their place. A hulking figure emerged from the forest, clad in dark, spiked armor. His eyes glowed crimson, and a massive axe rested on his shoulder. He pointed toward the tower, his guttural voice carrying over the battlefield.

"Bring me the girl and the stone!"

Amara's blood ran cold as the figure charged forward, cutting down villagers with brutal efficiency. Kael moved to intercept him, their blades clashing in a shower of sparks. The ground shook with the force of their blows, and for the first time, Kael seemed to struggle.

"Stay here," Oran commanded, stepping forward to aid Kael. His staff unleashed a burst of light, forcing the armored figure back momentarily.

Amara could not stand by any longer. The Bloodstone's power thrummed in her veins, and she knew what she had to do. She sprinted toward the fight, ignoring Lyra's shout of protest.

As she reached the edge of the battlefield, the armored figure turned toward her, a wicked grin spreading across his scarred face. "Ah, the chosen one," he sneered. "Let's see what you're made of."

Amara held the Bloodstone high, its light blazing against the dawn. "You want it? Come and take it."

The figure lunged, his axe swinging toward her. At the last moment, Amara raised her free hand, channeling the Bloodstone's power. A barrier of light erupted between them, the force of it sending him staggering back.

Kael seized the opportunity, his blade driving into the chink in the figure's armor. The man roared in pain, his axe falling from his grasp. Amara felt the Bloodstone's energy surge again, and she directed it toward Kael, strengthening him for the final blow.

With a mighty swing, Kael's sword cleaved through the armored figure, who crumpled to the ground. Silence fell over the battlefield as the remaining soldiers of the Crimson Order hesitated, then fled back into the forest.

The aftermath was grim. The village square was littered with the wounded and the dead, the air heavy with the stench of blood and smoke. But they had won—for now.

Oran approached Amara; his face lined with exhaustion but his eyes full of pride. "You've taken your first step toward mastering the

Bloodstone," he said. "But this is only the beginning. The Order will return, stronger than before."

Kael joined them, his armor splattered with blood. "Then we'll be ready." He looked at Amara, his expression softening. "You were incredible."

Amara managed a tired smile, her legs trembling beneath her. "I had help."

As the villagers began to regroup, tending to the wounded and repairing what they could, Amara felt the Bloodstone's pulse steadying, its energy still thrumming within her. The battle was over, but the war had only just begun.

Chapter 11

The sun dipped low over the horizon, painting the sky in shades of fire and amber. The villagers worked tirelessly to clean the wreckage of the Crimson Order's attack; their faces grim but resolute. Amara stood in the shadow of the tower, the Bloodstone pulsing softly against her chest.

Kael approached; his steps heavy but measured. His armor bore the scars of battle—gouges and dents that mirrored the exhaustion in his eyes. "The villagers are regrouping. They will fight, but they are shaken."

"They fought bravely," Amara replied, her voice soft. "But they shouldn't have to keep sacrificing for something they don't fully understand."

"They know what's at stake," Kael said firmly. "The Bloodstone's power is not just for you. It is for all of us."

Amara turned away, her gaze falling to the village square. The bodies of fallen villagers and crimson soldiers had been moved to the edges, but the memory of their faces lingered. The weight of the Bloodstone seemed heavier than ever.

Oran joined them, his staff clicking softly against the cobblestones. "The village's defenses will not hold against another assault like this. We need allies, and we need them quickly."

"Where do we find allies in a world that fears or envies the Bloodstone?" Amara asked.

Oran's expression was unreadable. "Not all who fear it seek to destroy it. There are whispers of a nomadic pack in the northern tundra—wolves who have rejected the Crimson Order's rule. They may be willing to help, if we can prove ourselves worthy."

Kael's brow furrowed. "The tundra's no place for amateurs. Even seasoned fighters have been lost to its storms."

Amara stepped forward, determination hardening her voice. "Then it is a risk we take. We cannot stand alone against the Order."

Kael's gaze lingered on her, a mixture of admiration and frustration in his crimson eyes. Finally, he nodded. "Then we leave at first light. But we are not just walking into the tundra unprepared."

The next morning, the trio stood at the village's edge, their packs laden with supplies. Lyra approached; her bow slung across her back. "You'll need a scout," she said without preamble.

Kael frowned. "You're needed here."

"The villagers can handle themselves," she replied, her tone sharp. "Besides, you will need someone who knows the terrain. The tundra's a death trap for the unprepared."

Amara glanced at Kael, who sighed but did not argue. "Fine," he said. "But you follow orders."

Lyra smirked. "Sure, Alpha."

The journey to the tundra was grueling. The forest gave way to barren plains, and the temperature dropped steadily as they pressed northward. By the time they reached the tundra's edge, the landscape was an endless expanse of white, broken only by jagged ice formations that jutted skyward like frozen spears.

The cold bit through Amara's cloak, but the Bloodstone's warmth offered some comfort. As they trudged forward, she felt its pulse quicken, as if responding to something unseen.

"What is it?" Kael asked, noticing her hesitation.

"I don't know," Amara admitted. "The Bloodstone... it feels different here. Stronger."

Oran's eyes narrowed. "The tundra is an ancient place, rich with elemental energy. The Bloodstone may be reacting to it. Stay alert."

By nightfall, they reached a cluster of ice caves nestled at the base of a frozen cliff. The caves offered some shelter from the howling wind, but the air inside was eerily still. Kael built a small fire, its flickering light casting long shadows on the icy walls.

As they settled in, a low growl echoed from deeper within the cave. Everyone froze. Lyra's hand flew to her bow, Kael's sword gleamed in the firelight, and Oran's staff hummed faintly with energy.

A pair of golden eyes appeared in the darkness, followed by another, and then another. Wolves—massive and silver-furred—emerged from the shadows, their movements fluid and predatory. They surrounded the group, their teeth bared.

A figure stepped forward, taller than the wolves and cloaked in furs. His face was sharp, his eyes an unsettling mix of gold and gray. "You tread on sacred ground," he said, his voice a deep rumble. "Why are you here?"

Amara stepped forward, the Bloodstone glowing faintly beneath her cloak. "We seek allies against the Crimson Order."

The man's eyes flicked to the Bloodstone, his expression hardening. "And you bring that cursed stone into our domain? Do you think us fools?"

"We think your survivors," Kael interjected. "Like us. The Order is hunting anyone who opposes them. You have fought them before; you know what they are capable of."

The man studied Kael, then Amara, his gaze lingering on the Bloodstone. "The Order is relentless, but so are we. If you wish for our help, you must prove you are worthy of it."

"How?" Amara asked.

The man's lips curved into a faint, wolfish smile. "The tundra will decide."

Before anyone could react, the wolves surged forward, their growls filling the air. Amara raised the Bloodstone instinctively, its light blazing as a barrier formed around them. The wolves recoiled, but the man only laughed.

"Clever," he said. "But light alone will not save you. Show me your strength."

Kael stepped forward; his sword gleaming. "We'll show you strength."

The man's smile widened. "Good. Then let the trial begin."

The icy ground beneath them shifted, and a chilling wind howled through the cave, carrying with it the sound of distant howls. Amara's heart pounded as she gripped the Bloodstone, its power surging in response to the challenge ahead.

The trial of the tundra had begun.

Chapter 12

The wolves' howls echoed through the icy caverns, mingling with the biting wind that swept through the frozen expanse. Amara's breath fogged the air as she clutched the Bloodstone, its warmth fighting against the numbing cold. Around her, Kael, Oran, and Lyra prepared for whatever was to come.

The pack leader, still cloaked in furs, gestured toward the mouth of the cave. "The tundra will test your resolve, your strength, and your unity. Survive, and you will earn our aid. Fail, and the tundra will claim you."

"Is this some kind of game to you?" Kael growled, his grip tightening on his sword.

The leader's golden-gray eyes flicked to Kael, unamused. "The tundra's trials are no game. They are sacred. If you cannot endure them, you cannot hope to stand against the Crimson Order."

Without another word, he stepped back into the shadows, his wolves following silently. The group was left standing at the cave's entrance, the icy wind howling outside.

The first challenge began the moment they stepped onto the frozen tundra. The ground beneath their feet cracked and shifted, revealing a series of narrow ice bridges spanning a vast chasm. Below, a swirling void of icy mist obscured whatever lay at the bottom.

Lyra whistled low. "Great. Death by falling is not exactly my ideal trial."

"Stay focused," Oran warned, his staff glowing faintly to light the way. "The tundra thrives on distraction. It will exploit any weakness."

Kael tested the first bridge, his heavy boots crunching against the brittle ice. It held, but just barely. "One at a time," he said, motioning for Amara to follow.

Amara hesitated, the Bloodstone pulsing in her hand as if sensing her fear. "What if it gives out?"

"It won't," Kael said firmly. "Trust yourself."

Taking a deep breath, Amara stepped onto the ice. The bridge swayed beneath her, the wind threatening to topple her with every step. She focused on the Bloodstone's warmth, using it to steady her nerves. When she reached the other side, Kael extended a hand to help her off the bridge.

"See? You are stronger than you think," he said.

The others crossed in turn, Lyra moving with practiced ease while Oran used his staff to stabilize the ice. As they regrouped, the ground rumbled ominously. Behind them, the bridges shattered, leaving no path of retreat.

"No turning back now," Lyra muttered.

The second trial came as a blinding snowstorm that swept across the tundra without warning. The wind howled with a deafening fury, and the temperature plummeted. Amara could barely see Kael, who was only a few paces ahead, his figure obscured by the swirling snow.

"We need to stay together!" Oran shouted; his voice barely audibles over the storm. He raised his staff, its light forming a faint dome around them.

The storm seemed almost alive, its icy tendrils clawing at the barrier. Amara felt the Bloodstone pulse urgently, as if urging her to act. She closed her eyes, focusing on its energy. Slowly, she extended her will outward, envisioning a shield to bolster Oran's magic.

The dome brightened, and the storm's fury lessened slightly. But the effort was draining, and Amara's legs trembled beneath her. "I can't hold it much longer," she said through gritted teeth.

Kael stepped beside her, placing a steadying hand on her shoulder. "You do not have to do it alone. Let us share the burden."

Amara nodded, releasing some of the Bloodstone's power to flow through the group. Lyra's sharp eyes found a faint outline of shelter—a cluster of ice spires just visible through the storm. Together, they pushed forward, their combined strength keeping the storm at bay until they reached the spires.

The final trial was the most harrowing. Deep within the spires, they found a massive frozen lake. At its center stood a pedestal, and atop it, a shard of glowing ice that pulsed with an otherworldly light. The air around the shard crackled with energy.

"That's it," Oran said, his voice reverent. "The Heart of the Tundra. It is what binds this land and its magic. To prove ourselves, we must claim it."

"Let me guess," Lyra said dryly. "There's a catch."

As if in answer, the ice beneath their feet groaned, and massive creatures emerged from the lake—golems of ice and frost, their eyes glowing with cold fire. They moved with surprising speed, their limbs leaving trails of frost in the air.

Kael drew his sword, its blade gleaming as he charged the nearest golem. "Protect Amara! She is the only one who can claim the shard!"

The battle was chaotic. Lyra's arrows shattered against the golems' icy hides, while Oran's magic slowed their movements but could not stop them entirely. Kael fought fiercely, his blade cutting through the creatures with powerful, deliberate strikes. But for every golem that fell, another rose from the lake.

Amara sprinted toward the pedestal, the Bloodstone blazing in her hand. The golems seemed to sense her intent, turning their attention toward her. Lyra lost a flurry of arrows, drawing their focus, while Oran unleashed a blinding burst of light to clear her path.

Reaching the pedestal, Amara placed the Bloodstone against the shard. A surge of energy coursed through her, the shard's icy magic merging with the Bloodstone's fiery power. The two forces intertwined, creating a brilliant pulse that radiated outward.

The golems froze in place, their glowing eyes dimming as they crumbled into piles of snow and ice. The lake stilled, and an eerie silence fell over the tundra.

The pack leader emerged from the shadows, his wolves at his side. He studied Amara, his expression unreadable. "You have passed the trial. The Heart of the Tundra recognizes your strength and your unity."

Amara's legs buckled, and Kael caught her before she could fall. The pack leader approached, placing a hand over the Bloodstone. "The tundra's power is now yours to wield. Use it wisely."

"Does this mean you'll help us?" Kael asked.

The leader nodded. "We will fight with you. The Crimson Order will not stand against the strength of the tundra."

As the group made their way back to the cave, Amara felt the Bloodstone's pulse steady, its power stronger than ever. They had earned the wolves' alliance, but the war was far from over.

Chapter 13

The journey back to the village was both a relief and a challenge. The tundra's biting cold eased only slightly with the wolves' guidance. Amara walked in silence, her fingers brushing the Bloodstone beneath her cloak. The shard from the Heart of the Tundra had merged with the stone, amplifying its power but also deepening the weight of responsibility she felt.

Kael stayed close, his eyes scanning the horizon. "You're quiet," he said, his voice low enough that the others could not hear.

Amara glanced at him. "Just thinking. The Bloodstone... it is stronger now, but it is also more unpredictable. I can feel it—the power is growing, but so is its pull. What if I cannot control it?"

Kael's expression softened, a rare moment of vulnerability breaking through his usual stoicism. "You are not alone in this. We are with you. Whatever happens, we will face it together."

She nodded, his words providing a flicker of comfort. Behind them, Oran and Lyra walked with the wolves, the tension between them and their newfound allies gradually easing. The pack leader, who had introduced himself as Fenrik, remained at the front, his commanding presence unshaken by the arduous journey.

When they reached the outskirts of the village, the sight that greeted them was one of grim determination. The villagers had rebuilt what they could, reinforcing their defenses and preparing for another assault. Their faces lit up when they saw Amara and her group, followed by expressions of awe and unease at the sight of the wolves.

Elder Maren hobbled forward, her keen eyes narrowing as they fell on Fenrik. "So, the whispers were true. The wolves of the tundra still walk among us."

"And now we fight alongside you," Fenrik replied, his voice steady. "But do not mistake our presence for submission. We aid you because the Crimson Order threatens all who value freedom."

Maren's gaze shifted to Amara. "You have done well, child. But this alliance will bring challenges of its own. The wolves' ways are not ours."

"We don't have to understand each other completely to fight for a common cause," Amara said. "Right now, we need every ally we can get."

The elder's eyes softened. "Spoken like a true leader."

That evening, the village gathered to welcome their new allies. A fire roared in the center of the square, its warmth a stark contrast to the icy tundra they had left behind. Amara sat with Kael, Oran, and Lyra, listening as Fenrik recounted tales of the wolves' battles against the Crimson Order.

"They've hunted us for years," Fenrik said, his golden-gray eyes reflecting the firelight. "But they have yet to break us. The tundra teaches resilience, and we have learned to endure where others would fall."

"Why haven't you fought back more directly?" Lyra asked. "With your strength, you could do some serious damage."

Fenrik's expression darkened. "Direct attacks come at a cost. For every blow we strike, they retaliate tenfold, targeting those who cannot defend themselves. We have chosen our battles carefully, but with the Bloodstone on your side, the balance may shift."

Amara felt the weight of his words. The Bloodstone had already changed so much, and its power continued to grow. But with that power came danger—not just to her, but to everyone around her. She glanced at Kael, who gave her a reassuring nod, as if sensing her thoughts.

Later that night, Amara found herself unable to sleep. She wandered to the edge of the village, where the wolves had set up camp. Fenrik stood apart from his pack, his gaze fixed on the moonlit forest.

"Can't sleep either?" she asked, approaching cautiously.

He did not turn but acknowledged her with a slight nod. "The Bloodstone calls to you, doesn't it?"

Amara hesitated. "How do you know?"

"I have seen its kind before. Relics of great power often carry voices—some that guide, others that deceive. The question is, which voice will you follow?"

She shivered, not from the cold but from the weight of his words. "I do not know. Sometimes it feels like it is helping me, but other times... it is like it has a will of its own."

Fenrik finally turned to face her, his eyes piercing. "Then you must master it before it masters you. The Bloodstone may be a weapon, but it is also a living thing. Respect it, but never let it control you."

Amara nodded slowly, his advice settling heavily on her mind. As she returned to the village, she could not shake the feeling that the trials were far from over. The Bloodstone had brought them allies and strength, but it had also painted a target on their backs. The Crimson Order would not rest, and neither could she.

Tomorrow, the battle would begin anew, and Amara would need every ounce of courage and resolve to face what lay ahead.

Chapter 14

The village remained quiet under the blanket of midnight. The distant howls of the wolves echoed faintly through the forest, their watchful presence a strange comfort. Amara leaned against the wooden railing of the makeshift watchtower; her gaze fixed on the stars above. The Bloodstone pulsed faintly at her side, as though it, too, was restless.

"You're supposed to be resting." Kael's voice broke through the stillness, soft and familiar. She turned to see him ascending the ladder, his tunic loose and his sword absent for once. His expression was softer than usual, his usual edge replaced by something gentler.

"Couldn't sleep," she admitted, brushing her hair out of her face as the wind picked up. "Too much on my mind."

Kael stepped onto the platform, his broad frame seeming to take up all the space. He leaned on the railing beside her, his arm brushing hers. The warmth of his presence was grounding, a stark contrast to the chill in the air.

"You've done more in these past weeks than most would dare in a lifetime," he said. "It's okay to let yourself breathe once in a while."

Amara sighed, the weight of his words sinking in. "Every time I close my eyes, I see them—the Crimson Order, the destruction they have caused. I cannot stop thinking about what happens if we fail."

Kael turned to face her fully, his hand finding hers on the railing. His touch was firm, steadying. "We will not fail. Not if we are together."

She looked up at him, her breath catching at the intensity in his eyes. The moonlight softened his sharp features, highlighting the vulnerability hidden beneath his usual stoicism. For a moment, the world around them faded, leaving only the two of them.

"You're always so sure," she said softly, her voice barely above a whisper.

Kael's lips quirked into a small smile. "Not always. But when it comes to you, Amara, I have never been more certain of anything."

The distance between them disappeared as he stepped closer, his hand moving to cup her cheek. Amara's heart raced, her pulse quickening under his touch. She tilted her face toward him, her resolve slipping as the moment stretched.

"Kael," she breathed, her voice trembling with unspoken emotion.

He silenced her with a kiss, his lips capturing hers in a way that was both tender and insistent. The Bloodstone pulsed faintly at her side, its warmth mingling with the heat that bloomed between them. Amara's hands found their way to his chest, her fingers curling into the fabric of his tunic as she leaned into him.

Time seemed to stand still as the kiss deepened, the tension that had been building between them finally breaking free. Kael's arms wrapped around her, pulling her close as if he could shield her from the weight of the world. Amara surrendered to the moment, letting herself forget the trials and dangers that awaited them, if only for a little while.

When they finally parted, their foreheads rested together, their breaths mingling in the cool night air. Kael's hand lingered on her waist, his thumb tracing slow, soothing circles.

"We should get back," Amara said reluctantly, though she made no move to pull away.

"In a moment," Kael murmured, his voice a low rumble that sent shivers down her spine. "Just... stay a little longer."

Amara nodded, her eyes closing as she let herself savor the rare peace they had found in each other. For the first time in what felt like forever, she allowed herself to hope—not just for victory, but for the possibility of something more.

The dawn came too soon, bringing with it the reality of their mission. But as Amara and Kael descended from the watchtower, their bond felt stronger than ever. Whatever lay ahead, they would face it together.

Chapter 15

As dawn broke over the village, the air carried a sense of foreboding. The wolves had returned to their positions along the perimeter, their keen eyes scanning the forest. The villagers moved with purpose, reinforcing barricades, and preparing for the inevitable confrontation with the Crimson Order. Amara stood at the center of the square, her cloak whipping in the wind as she addressed the crowd.

"We have little time," she began, her voice steady despite the storm of emotions churning within her. "The Crimson Order knows of the Bloodstone's power. They will come for it, and when they do, we must be ready."

Fenrik stepped forward, his presence commanding as he addressed the villagers. "We fight together. My pack will defend the forest, ensuring no enemy slips through. But the battle will be won or lost here. Trust in each other, and trust in your strength."

Kael placed a reassuring hand on Amara's shoulder as murmurs of agreement rippled through the crowd. "They'll follow you," he said quietly. "You've already shown them what's possible."

Amara nodded, drawing strength from his words. "Then we'll give them a reason to believe."

The hours leading up to the battle were a blur of activity. Amara moved between groups, offering guidance and encouragement as the villagers and wolves worked side by side. Oran and Lyra organized the archers, while Kael oversaw the construction of additional defenses. Fenrik and his wolves patrolled the outskirts, their movements fluid and precise.

In a quiet moment, Amara retreated to the elder's hut, where the Bloodstone lay on a makeshift altar. Its surface shimmered with an otherworldly light, the faint hum of its power filling the room. She placed her hands on the stone, closing her eyes as she reached out to it.

The connection was immediate and overwhelming. Visions of fire and blood filled her mind, the cries of battle blending with the relentless pulse of the stone. Yet beneath the chaos, she sensed something else—a thread of clarity, a voice that whispered of strength and unity.

"Amara."

She opened her eyes to find Elder Maren standing in the doorway, her expression grave. "The Bloodstone's power grows with you, but so does the danger. You must be careful not to lose yourself to it."

Amara straightened, her resolve firm. "I will do whatever it takes to protect them. The Bloodstone is our best chance."

The elder nodded, her gaze softening. "Just remember, its power is a tool, not a crutch. Trust in your own strength as much as the stone's."

As twilight descended, the first signs of the enemy's approach became evident. The forest grew unnaturally still, the usual sounds of wildlife replaced by an eerie silence. The wolves' howls pierced the air, signaling the arrival of the Crimson Order.

Amara stood at the front line, her heart pounding as the enemy emerged from the shadows. Clad in dark armor, their ranks moved with precision, their crimson banners billowing in the wind. At their center was a figure shrouded in black, a sinister aura emanating from them.

"That's him," Kael said, his voice low. "The commander."

Amara's grip tightened on her staff as she felt the Bloodstone's power surge within her. She stepped forward, her voice ringing out across the battlefield.

"You've come for the Bloodstone," she called, her tone unwavering. "But you'll find only defeat here."

The commander laughed, a cold, hollow sound that sent a chill through the air. "Brave words for someone so outmatched. Surrender the stone, and I may spare your lives."

"We'll never surrender," Amara replied, her voice firm. "This ends here."

The commander raised a gauntleted hand, and the Crimson Order surged forward. The battle began in a cacophony of steel and cries, the village's defenders meeting the enemy with fierce determination. Arrows rained down from the rooftops, and the wolves darted through the chaos, their fangs and claws tearing through the enemy ranks.

Amara fought with a precision and ferocity she had not known she possessed, the Bloodstone's power coursing through her. Each strike of her staff sent waves of energy rippling through the battlefield, driving back the Crimson Order. But with every use of the stone's power, she felt its pull grow stronger, its whispers more insistent.

"Focus, Amara!" Kael shouted, cutting down an enemy who had slipped through the defenses. "Don't let it take over!"

She nodded, forcing herself to remain grounded as she fought. Around her, the tide of battle shifted, the villagers and wolves holding their ground despite the overwhelming odds. Yet she knew the fight was far from over. The true test was still to come.

Chapter 16

The battle's chaos unfolded around Amara like a storm, a whirlwind of screams, steel, and shadows. The Crimson Order's commander stood unmoved amidst his soldiers, exuding a chilling presence that seemed to warp the air. Every clash of weapons, every arrow loosed, every howl of the wolves echoed with the weight of fate.

Amara's heart pounded as she carved her way through the throng of enemies, her staff a blur of energy and precision. The Bloodstone's pulse matched her movements, each swing imbued with raw, devastating power. But with each strike, the whispers grew louder, urging her to unleash more, to surrender to the overwhelming force within.

"Amara!" Kael's voice pierced through the din. He fought his way to her side, his sword flashing as he dispatched an armored foe. Blood streaked his face, but his focus remained unwavering. "We are being pushed back. The barricades will not hold much longer."

Amara nodded; her breaths ragged. "We need to get to the commander. This will not end until he is stopped."

Kael's jaw tightened, his gaze flickering to the imposing figure in the distance. "I will clear a path. You focus on him—but do not let the Bloodstone take you too far."

Together, they surged forward, cutting through the Crimson Order's ranks with a deadly efficiency. Fenrik and his wolves joined the fray, their savage precision turning the tide in places where the line wavered. The pack leader growled an acknowledgment as he leaped past Amara, his fangs tearing into an enemy soldier.

Amara's path to the commander became clearer with each step, the battlefield narrowing in her focus. The Bloodstone thrummed, its power growing more insistent, more intoxicating. She could feel its energy coursing through her veins, urging her to strike, to destroy, to end the threat once and for all.

Finally, she stood before him. The commander turned to face her, his armor gleaming darkly in the firelight. His eyes glowed a menacing crimson, and a cruel smile curled his lips.

"The wielder of the Bloodstone," he said, his voice a deep, resonant echo. "You are stronger than I anticipated. No matter. The stone's power will soon be mine."

Amara gripped her staff tighter, her knuckles white. "You'll never have it," she said, her voice steady despite the storm raging within her.

The commander raised his hand, summoning a torrent of dark energy that lashed out toward her. Amara moved instinctively, the Bloodstone's power surging as she raised a shield of light to deflect the attack. The force of the collision sent shockwaves through the battlefield, knocking soldiers from both sides off their feet.

"You can't control it forever," the commander taunted, stepping closer. "The stone will consume you. And when it does, you will beg for me to take it."

Amara ignored his words, focusing on the energy coursing through her. She countered his next attack with a burst of power that sent him staggering back. The whispers in her mind grew louder, more demanding. Use it all, they urged. End this now.

Kael's voice rang in her memory: *Do not let it take over.*

With a deep breath, she pushed back against the stone's pull, channeling its energy into precise, controlled strikes. The commander's attacks grew more erratic as he realized she was not succumbing to the stone's influence. His confidence wavered, his movements becoming desperate.

"This is for everyone you've hurt," Amara said, her voice firm. She gathered the Bloodstone's energy for one final blow, her staff glowing with an intense, radiant light. The commander raised his hands to defend himself, but it was too late. The force of her strike shattered his defenses, sending him sprawling to the ground.

The battlefield fell silent as the remaining soldiers of the Crimson Order froze, their leader's defeat robbing them of their resolve. Fenrik's wolves pressed the advantage, driving the enemy back until they broke into a full retreat.

Amara stood over the commander, her chest heaving with exertion. The Bloodstone's whispers quieted; their urgency replaced by a strange, heavy calm. Kael approached, his sword still at the ready as he assessed the fallen enemy.

"It's over," he said, though his tone carried a note of caution.

Amara nodded, lowering her staff. "For now." She looked out over the battlefield, where villagers and wolves tended to the wounded and reinforced their defenses. The victory felt hard-won, but she knew their fight was not truly over.

The Bloodstone's pulse reminded her of that. Its power had saved them, but its cost loomed over her like a shadow. For now, she had won—against the Crimson Order, and against the stone's pull. But the true test of her strength was only beginning.

Chapter 17

The morning sun barely pierced through the dense gray clouds gathering over the village, casting an ominous shadow on the land. The air was thick with tension as villagers and wolves alike worked tirelessly to rebuild what had been lost. Amara stood at the edge of the village square, observing the activity while her mind raced with the implications of the Crimson Order's retreat. They had not been defeated; they were biding their time.

Kael approached; his movements brisk. "The scouts are back," he said, his voice low. "You'll want to hear this."

Amara followed him to the makeshift war council assembled in the elder's hut. Fenrik, Elder Maren, and several of the senior warriors were gathered around a crude map of the region. The scouts—a wiry man named Rhen and a swift-footed wolf named Larka—stood before the group, their expressions grim.

"What did you find?" Amara asked, stepping into the circle.

Rhen exchanged a glance with Larka before speaking. "The Crimson Order has set up a stronghold in the old ruins beyond the eastern ridge. They're gathering reinforcements—mercenaries, beasts, and something else."

Larka's fur bristled as she added, "We felt it. Dark magic, thick and unnatural. Whatever they're planning, it's coming soon."

A heavy silence fell over the room. Amara's hand instinctively went to the Bloodstone beneath her cloak. Its warmth was a constant reminder of its presence, and its whispers began to stir once more.

Elder Maren broke the silence. "We cannot wait for them to strike. If we allow them to amass their forces, we'll be overwhelmed."

Fenrik growled in agreement. "We'll need to strike first. Take the fight to them while they're still vulnerable."

Kael leaned over the map, tracing a route with his finger. "If we move quickly, we can reach the ruins before nightfall. A small, agile force could infiltrate their camp and sabotage their defenses."

Amara's mind raced, weighing their options. The risk was immense, but so was the threat. She looked up, meeting the eyes of those around her. "We'll need our best fighters and our sharpest minds. This mission will be dangerous, but it's our best chance to stop them before it's too late."

Fenrik nodded. "My pack will join the strike team."

Kael placed a hand on her shoulder. "And you won't go without me."

Amara's gaze softened for a moment, but she quickly steeled herself. "We leave at midday. Prepare yourselves."

As the sun reached its zenith, the strike team gathered at the edge of the forest. Amara stood at the forefront, her staff in one hand and the Bloodstone pulsing beneath her cloak. Kael, Fenrik, Larka, and a dozen others formed the core of their group, their resolve evident in their determined expressions.

Before they set out, Elder Maren approached Amara. The elder's eyes were filled with a mix of pride and concern. "Remember, child, the Bloodstone is a tool, not a crutch. Trust in your own strength and in those who stand beside you."

Amara nodded, her heart heavy with the weight of responsibility. "I'll do what I must."

The journey to the ruins was tense but uneventful. The forest seemed to hold its breath as the strike team moved through the underbrush, their footsteps silent and their senses sharp. When they reached the edge of the eastern ridge, the ruins came into view.

Once a grand fortress, the ruins were now a dark and twisted shadow of their former glory. Crimson banners hung from crumbling walls, and the air was thick with the stench of death and decay. Figures moved within the stronghold; their forms distorted by the flickering light of unnatural flames.

Kael crouched beside Amara, his voice barely a whisper. "There's a gap in the wall to the north. We can slip in unnoticed if we're careful."

Amara nodded, signaling for the group to follow. They moved like shadows, slipping through the underbrush and into the gap Kael had pointed out. Inside, the stronghold was even more foreboding. Dark magic pulsed in the air, and the whispers of the Bloodstone grew louder, clawing at Amara's mind.

As they navigated the labyrinthine corridors, they came across a chamber filled with arcane symbols and a massive cauldron at its center. The air shimmered with malevolent energy, and a robed figure chanted in a guttural language.

Amara signaled for the group to halt. She could feel the Bloodstone's power resonating with the dark magic in the chamber, and it took all her willpower to resist its pull. Turning to the others, she whispered, "This is the heart of their operation. We destroy this, and we cripple their plans."

Fenrik growled low. "Then let's end this."

The battle that erupted in the chamber was fierce and chaotic. The robed figure unleashed waves of dark magic, but Amara countered with the Bloodstone's light, her power clashing against his in a dazzling display of energy. Kael and the others fought valiantly, holding off waves of defenders while Fenrik and his wolves tore through their ranks.

As the robed figure fell, the cauldron began to crack, releasing a surge of energy that sent everyone sprawling. Amara staggered to her feet, the Bloodstone's whispers now a deafening roar. She reached out with her power, channeling it into the cauldron and shattering it completely.

The resulting explosion rocked the ruins, and the strike team barely managed to escape as the stronghold collapsed behind them. Panting and bloodied, they regrouped in the forest, the distant howls of wolves signaling their retreat.

Amara clutched the Bloodstone, its glow dim but steady. The test was far from over, but for now, they had struck a decisive blow against the Crimson Order.

"This isn't the end," Kael said, his voice filled with both exhaustion and determination. "But it's a start."

Amara nodded, her resolve hardening once more. "We fight on. Together."

Chapter 18

The aftermath of the battle lingered like a storm that had yet to fully dissipate. The forest's stillness only amplified the echo of their escape from the ruins, and Amara's body still hummed with the Bloodstone's lingering energy. The group trudged through the dense underbrush in silence, each lost in their own thoughts as the remnants of dark magic clung to the air around them.

Kael, walking beside her, finally broke the quiet. "You should rest. You have been using the Bloodstone's power non-stop since the fight."

Amara's jaw tightened. "I'm fine."

"You're not fine," Kael said, his tone sharper now. "That thing—it is taking more from you than you realize. And if you are not careful, it will take all of you."

She stopped abruptly, turning to face him. The others paused, glancing back but giving the two a wide berth. "Do you think I don't know that?" she said, her voice low but trembling with suppressed anger. "Every time I use it, I feel it clawing deeper into my soul. But what choice do I have, Kael? This power is the only thing keeping us alive."

His gaze softened, but his frustration remained. "We need you, Amara. The real you. Not...whatever that stone is turning you into."

She stared at him for a long moment before sighing and looking away. "Let us keep moving. The village is not far."

When they finally emerged from the forest, the village was a hive of activity. The sight of returning warriors was met with cheers and relief, but the somber expressions on the strike team's faces quickly silenced the celebration. They had won a battle, but the war was far from over.

Elder Maren approached, leaning heavily on her staff. Her sharp eyes scanned the group, lingering on Amara. "You succeeded," she said, more a statement than a question.

Amara nodded. "The ruins are destroyed, and their forces scattered. But they will regroup. And when they do, they will be more dangerous than ever."

Maren's gaze darkened. "Then we must prepare. Come, all of you. We need to discuss what is next."

The war council convened in the central hall; the air thick with tension. Maps and notes cluttered the table, and every face around it bore the weight of the decisions they had to make. Fenrik spoke first, his voice a low growl. "We need to strike again, keep them on the defensive. If we give them time to regroup, we will lose the advantage."

Kael shook his head. "Our people are exhausted. Another attack now would risk everything."

"And waiting risks more," Fenrik countered, his claws raking lightly against the table. "You saw what they were summoning in that cauldron. Do you want to face whatever that was at full strength?"

Amara listened in silence, her fingers absently brushing the Bloodstone beneath her cloak. The whispers were faint now, but ever-present, like a shadow at the edge of her thoughts. Finally, she spoke. "We need information. Whatever the Crimson Order is planning, we need to understand it before we act. A hasty strike could play right into their hands."

Larka, who had been silent until now, nodded. "I can take a small team to scout their movements. Find out where they are regrouping and what they are planning."

Maren tapped her staff against the floor, drawing everyone's attention. "Then it is decided. Larka will lead a scouting party. The rest of us will focus on fortifying the village and preparing for whatever comes next."

The council dispersed, and Amara found herself alone outside the hall. The night air was cool, and the stars seemed dim against the inky black sky. She clutched the Bloodstone, its warmth a stark contrast to the chill around her.

"You're walking a dangerous path, child."

Amara turned to see Maren standing behind her, her expression unreadable. "I know," Amara said softly. "But I don't see another way."

Maren stepped closer, her gaze piercing. "The Bloodstone is a tool, yes. But it is also a curse. It will tempt you with power, but that power comes at a cost. Remember who you are, Amara. Do not let it consume you."

Amara nodded, though doubt gnawed at her heart. "I'll do my best."

Maren's hand rested briefly on her shoulder. "Your best will have to be enough."

As the elder walked away, Amara looked back up at the stars. The path ahead was fraught with danger and uncertainty, but she knew one thing for certain: she could not afford to falter. The fate of her people depended on it.

Chapter 19

The sun rose like a smear of fire on the horizon, bathing the village in pale orange light. Amara stood near the edge of the settlement, watching Larka and her scouting team gather their supplies. The air buzzed with an undercurrent of unease—a quiet acknowledgment that every decision now carried enormous weight.

"Are you sure you're ready?" Amara asked Larka as she adjusted the straps of her pack.

Larka flashed a confident grin. "I am always ready. Besides, someone must figure out what those crimson-cloaked bastards are up to."

Amara did not return the smile. Instead, she stepped closer and lowered her voice. "Be careful. If they are regrouping, it means they are dangerous—more dangerous than before. Do not take unnecessary risks."

"Relax, Alpha," Larka teased, though her tone held a hint of sincerity. "I will be back before you know it. Just keep Fenrik from sharpening his claws on someone while I am gone."

Amara could not help the faint smile that tugged at her lips. "Fine. Just do not make me come looking for you."

The group set off moments later, slipping into the woods like shadows. Amara watched until they vanished into the trees, unease settling like a stone in her stomach. Beside her, Kael appeared, silent but watchful.

"They'll be all right," Kael murmured.

Amara exhaled slowly. "I hope you are right. Because if they are not...we may not see what is coming next."

Kael's gaze drifted to the horizon, his expression darkening. "Then we'll have to be ready, no matter the cost."

Amara did not reply, but her hand drifted once again to the Bloodstone, its pulse echoing faintly against her palm.

Hours later, the village bustled with activity as defenses were reinforced. Warriors repaired walls, sharpened weapons, and trained tirelessly. Amara supervised, but her mind remained fixed on Larka's team. Shadows moved on the edge of her thoughts, whispers trailing just beyond comprehension. The Bloodstone was quiet, but she knew better than to trust its silence.

A sharp voice pulled her from her thoughts. "Alpha!"

She turned to see Fenrik rushing toward her, his brow furrowed. "What is it?"

"Larka's team...we've lost contact."

The world tilted for a heartbeat, then steadied as adrenaline surged through Amara. "How long?"

"Too long,"

Chapter 20

"They were supposed to send a signal back at noon—nothing came."

Amara did not waste time. "Gather a team. We will go after them."

Kael, who had been standing close by, stepped forward immediately. "I'm coming with you."

"No," Amara said firmly, though her tone softened at his glare. "You are needed here to hold the village together. If something happens to me or the others, you will have to lead."

Kael's frustration was evident, but he knew better than to argue. "Then take Fenrik."

Amara nodded, turning to Fenrik. "Meet me at the northern gate. We leave in ten minutes."

The forest seemed darker this time—each shadow stretched longer, and every rustling leaf sounded like a threat. Amara led the search party, her senses heightened, her grip on the Bloodstone tightening as they moved deeper into the woods.

Fenrik walked beside her, his sharp eyes scanning their surroundings. "If they ran into trouble, we will find them. They are strong."

"I know," Amara replied, though doubt still gnawed at her gut. Something felt *wrong*, and it was not just the silence of the forest. The Bloodstone pulsed faintly against her skin, as if warning her of something it would not name.

"Hold up," one of the warriors whispered, raising a hand to stop the group.

They halted. Amara strained her ears and caught it—a low, droning hum, unnatural and dissonant, like the rumble of something alive yet mechanical. The noise grew louder, and through the trees, flashes of red light began to flicker.

"Crimson magic," Fenrik growled.

Amara motioned for silence. "Fan out, but stay close. We do not know what we are walking into."

The group moved forward cautiously. Amara's heart pounded as the noise grew louder, vibrating in her chest. Finally, they broke through a dense wall of brush—and froze.

The clearing ahead was a scene of nightmares.

Larka's team was there—what remained of them. Bodies lay strewn across the ground, blood pooling into the dirt like ink. A crimson sigil burned in the center of the clearing, tendrils of red energy spiraling upward. Standing around it, hooded figures chanted in an ancient, guttural language, their hands outstretched toward the pulsating sigil.

And at the center of it all, suspended above the sigil, was *Larka*. She hung midair, her body limp, her face deathly pale. The red energy wrapped around her like a thousand strings, siphoning something vital from her body.

"No," Amara breathed, the Bloodstone burning against her chest.

Fenrik's claws extended, his voice a furious whisper. "What are they doing to her?"

Amara did not answer. The whispers in her mind surged, urging her to act. *Destroy them. Stop the ritual. Take the power for yourself.*

"Move in," she ordered, her voice low but resolute. "Take out the Crimson Order. Save Larka."

The warriors sprang into action. Fenrik led the charge, a blur of claws and fury as he tore into the nearest hooded figure. The chanting fractured into screams as the clearing erupted into chaos. Amara surged forward, the Bloodstone blazing in her hand, its energy flowing through her like molten fire.

"Amara!" Kael's voice echoed distantly in her mind, though she had not seen him in the chaos. "Don't—"

But she could not stop. The Crimson Order turned their attention to her, launching streams of crimson magic that crackled through the air. Amara threw up her hand, and a wall of shimmering energy exploded outward, deflecting their attacks. She felt the Bloodstone's hunger intensify, its whispers louder now.

More. Give me more.

One by one, the hooded figures fell. Amara barely noticed the warriors fighting beside her, barely registered the sound of Fenrik shouting her name. Her entire focus was on the sigil and on Larka—still suspended, still fading.

"Release her!" Amara screamed, lifting the Bloodstone. A shockwave of energy exploded from her palm, obliterating the sigil, and sending a ripple of magic across the clearing. The hooded figures collapsed like broken puppets; their bodies motionless.

Larka dropped.

Amara dashed forward and caught her before she hit the ground. "Larka! Larka, wake up."

Larka's eyes fluttered weakly, her voice a whisper. "Amara..."

"You're okay now," Amara said, though her voice shook. "You're safe."

Fenrik knelt beside them, his face grim. "We need to get her out of here. Now."

Amara nodded, clutching Larka tightly as the Bloodstone cooled against her skin. But as she looked back at the ruined sigil, dread settled deep in her bones.

This was no ordinary ritual. The Crimson Order was not just regrouping—they were summoning something.

And whatever it was, it was not finished yet. Fenrik said, his voice grave. "They were supposed to send a signal back at noon—nothing came."

Amara did not waste time. "Gather a team. We will go after them."

Kael, who had been standing close by, stepped forward immediately. "I'm coming with you."

"No," Amara said firmly, though her tone softened at his glare. "You are needed here to hold the village together. If something happens to me or the others, you will have to lead."

Kael's frustration was evident, but he knew better than to argue. "Then take Fenrik."

Amara nodded, turning to Fenrik. "Meet me at the northern gate. We leave in ten minutes."

The forest seemed darker this time—each shadow stretched longer, and every rustling leaf sounded like a threat. Amara led the search party, her senses heightened, her grip on the Bloodstone tightening as they moved deeper into the woods.

Fenrik walked beside her, his sharp eyes scanning their surroundings. "If they ran into trouble, we will find them. They are strong."

"I know," Amara replied, though doubt still gnawed at her gut. Something felt *wrong*, and it was not just the silence of the forest. The Bloodstone pulsed faintly against her skin, as if warning her of something it would not name.

"Hold up," one of the warriors whispered, raising a hand to stop the group.

They halted. Amara strained her ears and caught it—a low, droning hum, unnatural and dissonant, like the rumble of something alive yet mechanical. The noise grew louder, and through the trees, flashes of red light began to flicker.

"Crimson magic," Fenrik growled.

Amara motioned for silence. "Fan out, but stay close. We do not know what we are walking into."

The group moved forward cautiously. Amara's heart pounded as the noise grew louder, vibrating in her chest. Finally, they broke through a dense wall of brush—and froze.

The clearing ahead was a scene of nightmares.

Larka's team was there—what remained of them. Bodies lay strewn across the ground, blood pooling into the dirt like ink. A crimson sigil burned in the center of the clearing, tendrils of red energy spiraling upward. Standing around it, hooded figures chanted in an ancient, guttural language, their hands outstretched toward the pulsating sigil.

And at the center of it all, suspended above the sigil, was *Larka*. She hung midair, her body limp, her face deathly pale. The red energy wrapped around her like a thousand strings, siphoning something vital from her body.

"No," Amara breathed, the Bloodstone burning against her chest.

Fenrik's claws extended, his voice a furious whisper. "What are they doing to her?"

Amara did not answer. The whispers in her mind surged, urging her to act. *Destroy them. Stop the ritual. Take the power for yourself.*

"Move in," she ordered, her voice low but resolute. "Take out the Crimson Order. Save Larka."

The warriors sprang into action. Fenrik led the charge, a blur of claws and fury as he tore into the nearest hooded figure. The chanting fractured into screams as the clearing erupted into chaos. Amara surged forward, the Bloodstone blazing in her hand, its energy flowing through her like molten fire.

"Amara!" Kael's voice echoed distantly in her mind, though she had not seen him in the chaos. "Don't—"

But she could not stop. The Crimson Order turned their attention to her, launching streams of crimson magic that crackled through the air. Amara threw up her hand, and a wall of shimmering energy exploded outward, deflecting their attacks. She felt the Bloodstone's hunger intensify, its whispers louder now.

More. Give me more.

One by one, the hooded figures fell. Amara barely noticed the warriors fighting beside her, barely registered the sound of Fenrik shouting her name. Her entire focus was on the sigil and on Larka—still suspended, still fading.

"Release her!" Amara screamed, lifting the Bloodstone. A shockwave of energy exploded from her palm, obliterating the sigil, and sending a ripple of magic across the clearing. The hooded figures collapsed like broken puppets; their bodies motionless.

Larka dropped.

Amara dashed forward and caught her before she hit the ground. "Larka! Larka, wake up."

Larka's eyes fluttered weakly, her voice a whisper. "Amara..."

"You're okay now," Amara said, though her voice shook. "You're safe."

Fenrik knelt beside them, his face grim. "We need to get her out of here. Now."

Amara nodded, clutching Larka tightly as the Bloodstone cooled against her skin. But as she looked back at the ruined sigil, dread settled deep in her bones.

This was no ordinary ritual. The Crimson Order was not just regrouping—they were summoning something.

And whatever it was, it was not finished yet.

Chapter 21

Fenrik replied gravely. "They were supposed to check in hours ago."

Amara clenched her fists, forcing calm into her voice even as her mind raced. "Gather a team. We are going after them."

The forest was no longer a place of life and tranquility; it felt haunted, as though it recoiled from their presence. Amara led the search party with Fenrik by her side, her every sense on high alert. The Bloodstone throbbed beneath her cloak, as though it too sensed the shift in the air.

They moved in silence, the occasional snap of twigs or rustle of leaves setting nerves on edge. The deeper they went, the heavier the forest seemed, the light dimming unnaturally under the thick canopy.

"Over here!" one of the warriors called from ahead.

Amara's heart dropped as they approached. The scouting team's tracks were clear—signs of struggle scattered the ground. Weapons had been dropped; blood splattered the underbrush. But there were no bodies.

"They were taken," Fenrik said darkly, crouching over claw marks gouged into a tree. "Dragged deeper into the forest."

Amara did not hesitate. "We follow."

The trail led them to a massive clearing bathed in an unnatural crimson glow. At the center stood a colossal stone archway—ancient and pulsing with energy. Crimson-robed figures circled the arch, chanting in their guttural tongue. And beyond the arch, the air shimmered like a portal, revealing glimpses of a dark, shifting void.

Amara's breath caught as she spotted Larka and her team tied to stone pillars, their energy visibly draining into the portal. The sigils on the ground flared brighter as their life force fed into the dark magic.

"They're opening a gate," Fenrik growled. "Something's trying to come through."

Amara drew the Bloodstone, its surface blazing to life as if eager for what lay ahead. "We stop them. Now."

"Are you sure about this?" Kael's voice came from behind, his face grim as he stepped up to her. "If you use the Bloodstone again—"

"I know the risks," Amara cut him off. "But if we don't stop this, none of us will survive."

With a silent nod, Fenrik led the warriors into the fray, their battle cries shattering the air. Hooded figures turned, crimson magic exploding as the clash began. Amara did not wait; she sprinted toward Larka, her heart pounding.

"Hold on!" she shouted, slashing through two robed figures who moved to block her. The Bloodstone burned in her palm, its energy crackling outward and cutting a path to her trapped allies.

"Amara!" Larka's voice was weak, but alive. "You can't let it open!"

"I won't," Amara promised, already moving toward the archway. The Bloodstone flared with power, and she turned it on the swirling portal. Crimson tendrils shot toward her, dark and ravenous, but she met them head-on, her magic and will colliding with the forces spilling from the gate.

The forest shook violently. Amara screamed as the Bloodstone's energy surged through her, searing into her veins. It felt alive, demanding more—*demanding everything.*

"Amara, stop!" Kael shouted, his voice distant, panicked. "It'll kill you!"

She ignored him, pushing harder. The portal screamed back at her, a voice from the void—*ancient, monstrous, endless.* It tried to reach through, claws of darkness scraping at the edge of the world. But Amara did not yield. She could feel the Bloodstone's hunger, but she also felt her people—their hopes, their lives, their future.

"This is *my* power," she whispered, eyes blazing. "And I won't let you have them!"

With a final, agonized cry, she unleashed everything. The Bloodstone exploded with blinding light, obliterating the archway, the sigils, and the portal itself. The shockwave knocked everyone off their feet, the ground trembling as the void's grip shattered.

And then...silence.

Amara collapsed to her knees, the Bloodstone falling from her hand, its surface now dark and lifeless. She gasped for breath, her body trembling. Around her, the clearing slowly stilled. The Crimson Order lay scattered, defeated, their power broken. Larka and the others were freed, though weak and shaken.

Kael stumbled to her side, grabbing her shoulders. "Amara! Are you—"

"I'm fine," she whispered, though every part of her ached. She looked down at the Bloodstone, now just a dull stone. "It's over."

Back at the village, fires burned bright, and the air hummed with celebration. Larka and her team recovered, their ordeal behind them. Warriors swapped stories, and families reunited. For the first time in weeks, laughter returned.

Amara sat on the edge of the village wall, staring out at the dark forest. Kael joined her, silent for a moment before speaking. "You saved us."

She turned to him, exhaustion in her eyes. "We saved each other."

"And the Bloodstone?"

Amara looked down at her empty hand. "It is gone. Whatever it was, it is spent."

Kael studied her carefully. "Good. Maybe now you can rest."

"Maybe," she said softly. But as she looked out at the horizon, her thoughts lingered on the portal, on the dark void beyond it. The war had been won, but some battles were only the beginning.

For now, though, the village was safe. And for Amara, that was enough.

The End

Don't miss out!

Visit the website below and you can sign up to receive emails whenever D. Kepko publishes a new book. There's no charge and no obligation.

https://books2read.com/r/B-A-NIDAD-DFCLF

BOOKS 2 READ

Connecting independent readers to independent writers.

Also by D. Kepko

The Blood Moonstone

The Blood Moonstone
The Bloodstone Alpha

www.ingramcontent.com/pod-product-compliance
Lightning Source LLC
LaVergne TN
LVHW052051160826
845678LV00015B/3160

* 9 7 9 8 2 3 0 3 1 4 4 3 1 *